D1315863

Weekly Reader Books presents

The Thing in The Attic

by Charlotte Towner Graeber

(Original Title: The Thing in Kat's Attic)

pictures by Emily Arnold McCully

E. P. DUTTON   NEW YORK

This book is a presentation of Weekly Reader Books.
Weekly Reader Books offers book clubs for children from
preschool through high school.

For further information write to:
Weekly Reader Books
4343 Equity Drive
Columbus, Ohio 43228

Text copyright © 1984 by Charlotte Towner Graeber
Illustrations copyright © 1984 by Emily Arnold McCully

Library of Congress Cataloging in Publication Data

Graeber, Charlotte Towner.
The thing in Kat's attic.

Summary: After many tries, two young girls and their
mother finally discover what is making the mysterious
noises in their attic.
1. Children's stories, American. [1. Self-reliance—
Fiction. 2. Mothers and daughters—Fiction. 3. Single-
parent family—Fiction] I. McCully, Emily Arnold, ill.
II. Title.
PZ7.G75153Th 1984 [Fic] 84-8117
ISBN 0-525-44146-8

Published in the United States by E. P. Dutton, Inc.,
2 Park Avenue, New York, N.Y. 10016

Published simultaneously in Canada by
Fitzhenry & Whiteside Limited, Toronto

Editor: Julie Amper Designer: Isabel Warren-Lynch

Printed in the U.S.A. COBE First Edition
10 9 8 7 6 5 4 3 2 1

for Robyn, Birdie and Baby Bear

Contents

1
Clickety Skitch

Clickety click. Skitchety skitch.

Kat woke up. The bedroom was dark.

Clickety click. Skitchety.

There it was again. Kat sat up. *What* was that strange noise?

Her little sister, Holly, rolled over next to Kat.

Clickety click. Skitch skitch.

Where was that? Kat turned on the light. She looked up. The noise was coming from the ceiling. Something was moving around in the attic.

The light woke Holly up. She blinked her eyes. "Is it time to get up?" she asked.

"No," Kat whispered. "It's still nighttime."

Holly closed her eyes and rolled towards the wall. Then the noise came again. *Click click click.*

Holly popped up in bed. "What was that, Kat?" Her eyes were dark and wide.

"Nothing. I don't know. Go back to sleep," Kat said.

But it was too late. Holly pulled the covers over her head. Then she let out a wail. "Mommmm!"

First Putter, the dog, raced into the room. He jumped onto the bed and licked Holly's face. Then the hall light snapped on, and Mom came in.

"What's going on in here?" she asked. She pulled Putter off the bed.

"There's a monster in the attic! It's going to get us!" Holly yelled.

Mom shook her head. "There are no monsters. At least not here in New Albany." She turned to Kat. "What is this all about?" she asked.

Kat shrugged. "There were noises. Up there." She pointed to the ceiling.

Mom looked up. Putter jumped back on the bed. They all listened.

"I don't hear a thing," Mom said. "Are you sure you weren't imagining things?"

Just then: *Skitchety skitchety. Click.*

"That!" Kat jumped up. "That is what we heard!"

Holly ducked under the covers. Putter ran in circles at the foot of the bed. His nose was pointed towards the ceiling.

"*That* is just a mouse, I think," Mom said. She grabbed Putter and put him back on the floor. She uncovered Holly's head.

Clickety clickety. Skitch skitch.

Kat and Holly looked up at the ceiling.

"A noisy mouse," Mom said firmly.

"I wish Dad were here," Holly said. Her mouth curved into a pout.

Mom frowned. Then she sat down on the bed. "It's all right," she said. She pulled Kat and Holly into a hug. It was what Dad called a family hug. Only now it was just Mom and Holly and Kat.

"Try to get some sleep," Mom said at last. She stepped to the door with Putter right behind her.

"Can I sleep with you?" Holly asked.

"No. . . . But I'll leave the light on." Mom hugged them again. Then she went back to her own room.

Skitchety clickety. Click. Whatever it was ran across the attic floor.

Holly scooted to Kat's side of the bed. "I wish Dad still lived here," she whispered. "He'd know what to do." She tucked her feet under Kat's knees.

"It's probably just a mouse like Mom said," Kat said. "And Dad won't be here till Sunday, like always."

In a few minutes Holly was asleep. But Kat stared up at the dark ceiling—wide awake.

Skitch skitch skitch.

What was up there clickety skitching around? Was it a mouse like Mom said? It sounded too big! She wished Dad still lived with them, too.

2
Mousetraps

The next morning Mom got up late. She hurried Kat and Holly through breakfast. They all trundled out to the car.

Kat wished she were back in bed. She was still sleepy.

"Will the thing in the attic be gone tonight?" Holly asked.

"We'll set a trap—just to make sure," Mom said. "We'll stop at the hardware store on the way home."

Kat had seen mousetraps on TV cartoons. They always caught things by the tails. "Can't we just leave it in the attic, Mom?"

Mom shook her head. "Mice chew things. Insulation. Electrical wires. They could start a fire."

Still, a real trap could kill, thought Kat. "Maybe it will just go away by itself," she said.

Mom frowned at Kat. "I am going to catch the mouse. And that's that."

"My friend Bobby has a pet mouse," Holly said. "It lives in a hamster cage."

"No mouse—in the house—anywhere!" Mom said.

Mom left Holly at the day-care center. She dropped Kat off at school. In science class Mr. Bailey talked about fur-bearing mammals. Kat wondered about the noise in the attic. *Was* it only a mouse? And what was it *doing* up there?

After school Kat walked to the day-care center. At five thirty Mom picked them up. She drove to the hardware store.

Inside the store Kat and Holly followed Mom. She headed towards a clerk. He was stacking light bulbs on a shelf.

"Where are the mousetraps?" Mom asked.

The clerk turned. "Aisle eleven. To your right."

Mom took Holly's hand, and Kat followed them through the store. Aisle eleven was next to the paint section. Last fall Dad had taken Kat and Holly to pick out paint for their bedroom. They had chosen pale yellow. "Like lemon cream pie," Dad had said and laughed. It was his favorite dessert.

Now Mom stopped to study the shelves. At one end were pet supplies: dog chains, cat beds, flea powders, toys.

"Let's get a new ball for Putter," Holly said.

Mom ignored her. She walked to the middle of the aisle. "Here we are," she said. She leaned forward to look at the traps. Kat looked too.

Near the floor, huge cages made of wire took up two shelves. They were big enough to hold Putter. On a middle shelf, traps that said RAT CATCHER on the side filled two bins. They were made of wood with a wire spring on top. Kat knew the wire was supposed to snap down and catch the rat.

"Can I help you?" A clerk stood behind them. He wore a blue jacket.

Mom pointed to a bin on the top shelf. "I'll take two of these mousetraps," she said.

"Sure you want traps?" the clerk said. He glanced at Kat and Holly. "They're kind of messy."

Kat shivered.

"What choice do I have?" Mom asked.

The clerk reached for a yellow box. "Poison," he said. "No mess. They will just crawl away to die outside. No, uh—remains."

"No poison!" Mom said. "I don't want it in my house!"

The clerk shrugged and moved down the aisle. He picked up an orange and black box. "Just the thing!" he said. "The Supersonic Mouser!"

"Supersonic Mouser? What's that?" Kat asked.

"Electronic pest control," the clerk said. "Mousetrap of the future!"

Mom looked interested. "How does it work?"

"Electronic sound waves," the clerk said. "Sound drives them off, I guess."

Mom squinted at the box. "$49.95! Just to catch a mouse!"

The clerk put the box back on the shelf. And Mom moved back down the aisle to the bin of mousetraps.

"I think these will do," said Mom as she reached into the bin.

"I want a toy," Holly whined.

"I want to get home," Mom said.

Kat followed them to the checkout counter. She waited while Mom paid for the mousetraps and two lollipops—a red one for Kat, an orange one for Holly. Kat wished they could afford the Supersonic Mouser instead of the traps.

3
Mice Like Cheese

After supper Mom set the two mousetraps on the kitchen table. "Let's see. What do we have that a mouse would like to eat?" she said.

"Peanut butter," Kat said.

"Pizza!" Holly said. She was still eating a piece from supper.

"I think cheese will do just fine," Mom said.

Kat watched Mom place a small hunk on each mousetrap. Then Mom pulled back the wire springs.

"Stand back. I don't want any sore fingers."

"What about paws or tails?" Kat said.

"Enough of that," Mom warned. She set both traps aside. Then she carried the stepladder into the hallway.

"Are you going up *there?*" Holly asked.

"That's where the mouse is," Mom said. She placed the ladder under the trapdoor to the attic. Then she climbed up.

"I'll hold the ladder," Kat said. Mom always said that to Dad.

Kat sat on the floor holding the ladder legs. Holly sat next to her with Putter on her lap. Mom's head and shoulders disappeared through the opening.

"Doll dang it!" Mom backed down the ladder. "The light is burned out!"

Kat held the ladder tight.

Mom found a flashlight and climbed back up with the traps. Kat heard Mom bump across the attic. It sounded strange. Mom was bumping above their bedroom.

"Mom?" Kat called towards the trapdoor.

Holly sat on the floor with her fingers in her mouth.

In a few minutes Mom's feet and legs dangled through the opening. One foot found the top of the ladder. The other foot missed the second step down. Mom came sideways down the ladder and sat hard on the floor.

"Mom, are you all right?" Kat asked.

"Are you hurt?" Holly asked.

Putter licked Mom's cheek.

Mom's hair was full of cobwebs. Her jeans were dirty. "I'm all right. Just let me get my breath," Mom said. She brushed one hand through her hair and rubbed her knee.

Just then the door bell rang.

"I'll go," Kat said.

Holly followed, and they both looked through the door glass.

"Aunt Kathy!" Holly shrieked.

Kat opened the door. Aunt Kathy hugged Kat. She scooped Holly into her arms.

Then she stepped into the hallway. Mom was still sitting on the floor.

"What are you doing? Painting the ceiling?" Aunt Kathy asked.

"There is something in the attic," Kat said.

"A mouse," said Holly.

Aunt Kathy offered Mom her hand and helped her up. "What is a mouse doing in your attic?"

Mom folded the ladder and leaned it against the wall. "I don't *know* what it is doing up there," Mom said. "I just want to get it out."

"Mom put traps in the attic," Kat said.

"We put cheese in the traps," Holly said. "Mice like cheese."

Aunt Kathy shuddered.

"The reason I stopped by—" she said quickly. She pulled an envelope from her pocket. "Ta-da! Tickets to that play you wanted to see." She handed the envelope to Mom.

Mom took out two orange tickets. "You shouldn't have," she said. But her face beamed.

"It's time you had a night out," Aunt Kathy said. "Call a sitter. Iron your best dress."

"Oh, my! I haven't been to a play since . . ." Mom didn't finish.

But Kat knew what she meant—since Dad left. Kat remembered when Mom and Dad had gone out together almost every week.

That night Kat lay staring at the ceiling. Whatever was up in the attic was quiet now. Kat hoped it was not caught in a trap already.

4
A Better Trap

Skitchety skitch. Click click click.

Kat woke up. The bedroom was dark. The thing in the attic was moving around. It was not caught by its tail in one of the mousetraps.

Skitch clickety. Click.

Holly rolled over and groaned. But she didn't wake up. She pushed her feet against Kat's stomach.

Click click. Thump. Skitch skitchety.

Kat pulled the blanket over her head. But she could still hear the noises. The thing was running right over her head.

"Time to get up," Mom called from the hallway.

Kat opened her eyes. It was morning already. She didn't want to get up at all.

"Did we catch the mouse?" Holly asked.

Kat shook her head. "Something is still up there."

After breakfast Mom climbed into the attic. She brought down the mousetraps. The cheese was still there.

"Maybe it doesn't like cheese," Kat said.

"Maybe it likes pizza." Holly laughed.

Putter jumped at the traps in Mom's hand. He was after the cheese. One of the wires snapped at his nose.

"Wharauf!" Putter yelped.

"Poor Putter," Holly said. She cuddled him on her lap.

"That does it!" Mom said. "No more traps." Mom dumped the mousetraps in the garbage can.

Kat was worried. Something was in the attic. Something could chew on the electrical wires and start a fire. "What are we going to do now?" she asked.

"Let's call Dad," Holly said. "He'll know what to do."

"I'm sure we can catch a mouse without calling Dad," Mom said, and slammed the lid on the garbage can.

Kat wasn't so sure.

At school Kat worried about the chewing. What if a fire started in the attic while they were away? Putter was locked in the house and couldn't get out.

Mom picked up Kat and Holly at the regular time.

Kat climbed in the back seat of the car. "What is that?" she asked. A strange-looking cage lay on the floor.

Holly leaned over the front seat. "It's a cage."

"It's a special cage," Mom said. "One that catches animals without hurting them."

Kat studied the cage. She could not see how it worked. At one end it had a hinged wire door. At the other end there was a small metal tray on the bottom. How did the cage catch animals without hurting them?

"Where did you get it?" Holly asked.

"I borrowed it from the animal shelter," Mom said. "We can use it for ten days."

After supper Mom carried the cage into the kitchen. She put it in the middle of the floor.

"You put the food in the back of the cage," Mom explained. "On the metal tray."

Kat looked at the tray and nodded.

"Then you hook the door open, like this," Mom said. She hooked the door open.

"So the mouse can get in," Holly said.

"That's right," Mom said. "When he eats the food, the door closes and he can't get out." She pointed to a wire that attached the door to the tray.

"What happens after that?" Kat asked.

"We take the cage to the woods and open the door."

"And the mouse runs away," Holly said.

"If it *is* a mouse," Kat said.

Mom spread peanut butter on a slice of bread. Then

she placed it on the tray inside the cage. "I hope it likes peanut butter," she said.

Putter sniffed around the cage. But he wouldn't come too close. He remembered the snap of the mouse-trap on his nose.

Mom put the cage in the attic. "Now we're ready for our little friend," she said proudly.

Kat smiled. Mom *did* know what to do. They didn't need Dad to catch the thing in the attic.

5
Empty!

Click clickety. Skitch skitch clickety.
Kat woke up. Moonlight shone in the window.
Skitchety thump. Thump thump.
"Go into the cage. We don't want you in our attic,"
Kat whispered.
Holly rolled over. She pulled the covers with her.
Kat pulled them back again.
Thump thump. Clickety skitch. Back and forth.
Around and around. The thing in the attic sounded
like it was trying to get out.
The next morning Mom climbed into the attic. Kat
and Holly waited below. But nothing was in the cage.
The bread and peanut butter were still on the tray. The
door was still hooked open.
"Doll dang it!" Mom said.
"Maybe it doesn't like peanut butter," Holly said.

"Maybe it will be in the cage when we come home," Mom said. She took the cage back up.

That night Mom climbed into the attic as soon as they got home. She carried the cage down.

"Nothing," she said. In the kitchen she took out the bread and peanut butter.

Putter sat up and begged.

"Maybe it's not a mouse, and that's why it didn't eat," said Kat.

"Let's try something else," Mom said. She opened a bag of cookies and placed one in the cage. She gave a cookie to Holly and Kat—and one to Putter.

Mom put the cage back in the attic. Then she fixed supper: macaroni with tomatoes and cheese and peppers. Mom called it supperoni.

Holly did not like it. "Ugh! I don't want any!" she whined.

"Eat your supper," Mom said.

Kat knew what was coming next. Holly pushed the food around on her plate. But she would not eat.

Mom sighed. "You can try a few bites, Holly. You *like* macaroni."

"But I hate peppers," Holly sniffed. "Just like Dad. We never had supperoni when Dad was here."

Mom took a deep breath. "You may pick the peppers out."

Holly made a face and began picking at her meal. "I wish Dad were here," she mumbled.

"You will see your dad on Sunday," Mom said. She stood with her hands on her hips. "Now start eating."

Holly ate half of her supperoni. Mom scraped the rest into Putter's dish. Putter ate it all.

At seven thirty the doorbell rang. It was Aunt Kathy.

"Did you catch your mouse yet?" she asked.

Mom shook her head.

"I don't think it's a mouse," Kat said. "It didn't like cheese or bread and peanut butter, and it sounds too big."

"It could be a rat or a raccoon," Aunt Kathy said.

"How would it get in?" Mom asked. "It must be a mouse. They can get in anywhere."

"You should call an exterminator," Aunt Kathy said. "It could have rabies. What if it bites someone?"

"What's an exterminator?" Kat asked.

"Someone you pay to poison things for you," Mom said.

Aunt Kathy shrugged. "I'm only trying to help," she said.

"I know." Mom gave Aunt Kathy a hug. "But no poison. We can manage by ourselves, right Kat?"

"Right," Kat answered. But Kat did not know how they would manage. The thing in the attic would not go into the cage.

6

Nibby Nibby Crunch

Clickety thump. Clickety. Crunch crunch crunch.

Kat sat up in bed. The room was dark. She heard it again.

Crunch nibby nibby. Clickety click.

The thing in the attic was chewing! Maybe it was chewing the electrical wires. Maybe it was chewing through the ceiling and would fall right down on their heads. Kat slid out of bed and hurried to Mom's bedroom.

"Mom! Wake up!"

Mom sat up and turned on the light. "Kat. What's wrong?"

"It's chewing," Kat said. "I can hear it chewing right over my head!"

Mom put on her slippers and followed Kat back to her room. Kat turned on the light.

"It's coming to get me!" Holly wailed. She hid under the covers.

Mom pulled them off. "Nothing is going to get you," she said.

Thump thump. Clickety skitch skitch.

They all looked up. Putter sat on the foot of the bed.

"I don't hear any chewing," Mom said.

Suddenly: *Nibby nibby. Crunch nibby.*

"It *is* chewing," Mom said. "And it sounds too loud for a mouse!"

"I'm scared," Holly said. She scooted close to Mom. "I want it to go away."

Mom held Holly close. "Tell you what. You and Kat can sleep in my bed until morning."

"Where will you sleep?" Kat asked.

Thump thump clickety. Nibby crunch crunch.

Mom looked up. "I'll stay in here."

Kat led Holly back to Mom's room. They climbed into Mom's bed. Kat could not hear the noises now. She heard the soft ticking of Mom's clock on the dresser.

"I hope it doesn't get Mom," Holly said. She started to cry. "I don't want it up there. I want Dad to come and chase it away."

Kat rubbed Holly's back. She was too little to understand. Dad lived in the city now. They lived here. That was that.

The next morning the alarm woke Kat. She and Holly ran back to their own room. But Mom was not in their bed.

"Mom! Where are you?" Holly called.

"I'm up here!" Mom answered. Mom came down the ladder holding the flashlight. "I can hear it. But I can't see it," she said.

"Why doesn't it go in the cage?" Kat asked. "Why doesn't it eat the food on the tray?"

Mom shrugged. "I guess it's not hungry. There must be a hole where it can go in and out for food." She put on her coat. "I am going out to look."

"I couldn't see a hole," said Mom when she came back inside.

Just then someone knocked on the back door. Holly looked out the window.

"It's Mr. Mountain," she said.

Kat knew she meant Mr. Montayne, the man next door. Mom opened the door, and Mr. Montayne stepped inside.

"Saw you outside looking around. Anything wrong?" he asked.

Mom shook her head.

"There is something in our attic," Holly said. "A mouse—or a monster."

Mr. Montayne laughed. "Most likely a rat."

Mom poured milk on Holly's cereal.

"Be glad to smoke it out for you," Mr. Montayne said. "Either it gets out or it suffocates."

"Suffocate? What's that?" Kat asked.

Mr. Montayne's eyes narrowed. "The smoke clogs the air so things can't breathe."

Kat swallowed hard.

"We don't need any help," Mom said.

"It's no job for a woman," Mr. Montayne said. "Be glad to do it for you."

"No, thank you," Mom said firmly. She glanced at Kat and Holly. "We'll be just fine."

Mom followed Mr. Montayne to the door.

"There has to be an opening someplace. I know it," she said. "You and Holly get dressed now, Kat. I'll get the ladder and take a closer look."

Kat and Holly watched from the bedroom window. Mom set the ladder next to the house. Then she climbed up.

"What do you see?" Kat hollered out the window.

"Nothing!" Mom hollered back. "Get dressed!"

Kat and Holly dressed and watched at the same time.

Kat saw Mr. Montayne walk back across the yard. Everyone wanted to help get rid of the animal in the attic. Mr. Montayne wanted to suffocate it. Aunt Kathy wanted to call the exterminator. Kat wondered what Dad would do. Maybe Mom should call him after all.

7
No Help Needed

That night Mom set the cage on the kitchen floor. She placed an apple and a piece of cheese on the tray. Then she climbed into the attic.

"Maybe it doesn't want to get caught," Kat said.

Mom came down. "Maybe it likes causing us a lot of trouble." She leaned the ladder against the wall. "Maybe it likes living in our attic."

The next morning the cage was still empty. Mom left it in the attic.

That night Mom took Kat and Holly out to dinner. Kat ordered a cheeseburger. Holly ordered a plain hamburger with nothing on it—like always.

When they got home Kat and Holly watched Mom get ready to go to the play. Mom put on her heart-shaped earrings. Then she sprayed on her best perfume.

"Spray me," Holly said.

Mom sprayed behind Holly's ears.

"Spray me," Kat said.

Mom sprayed Kat's wrist. The perfume smelled like the spice bread from the bakery.

Mom put on her best dress and her shiny black shoes.

Aunt Kathy came to pick up Mom. She brought the sitter with her. It was Kat's cousin John.

"How is your monster in the attic?" Aunt Kathy asked.

"It's still there," Holly said.

"It is not a monster," Kat said. "It is a poor creature that wants out."

Mom shrugged. "Whatever it is, it's still there. But tomorrow is Saturday," she said. "I will get it out if it's the last thing I do."

"Let me know if you need any help," John said.

"We don't need any help," Mom said. "We are not a bunch of helpless women."

Aunt Kathy laughed. "Let's go."

"Have a good time and behave," Mom said.

Holly started to pout. Then Mom hugged her. "You can make popcorn and cocoa. You can play with my old shoes."

Holly ran off to Mom's closet. John and Kat sat down to play a game of Clue.

In the middle of the night, Kat heard Putter bark-

ing. She turned on the light. Putter stood on his hind legs beside the bed.

Thump thump. Nibby nibby crunch.

Putter jumped on the bed, and Holly woke up.

"It's getting louder," Holly said. She covered her ears.

Kat pulled Putter off the bed. She pushed him in the hall and shut the door.

Crunch crunch. Nibby crunch crunch.

"It's chewing up the house," Holly said. "I'm glad Dad is coming on Sunday."

Kat frowned at Holly. "What can Dad do?"

"I don't know," Holly said firmly. "But he'll do something."

Kat got back into bed and snapped off the light.

Clickety thump. Thump thump. The thing *was* getting louder.

"Don't worry, Holly," Kat said. "Mom is going to get it out if it's the last thing she does."

Kat liked Saturday breakfast. It meant pancakes or waffles or omelettes with cheese in them. But this morning Mom put a box of cereal on the table.

"I have work to do. You'll have to help yourselves," Mom said. She put on her coat.

"Did you bring me something?" Holly asked.

"After the play we went to a Chinese restaurant," Mom said. "I brought you each a fortune cookie."

Kat opened her cookie first and unrolled the tiny

36

"Where are you going?" Holly asked.

"I am going inside. Putter and I are going to chase the troublemaker out of our attic."

Holly sat down on the swing. Kat leaned against a tree. They both stared at the hole.

Mom waved out the open bedroom window. Then they heard Putter barking, and Mom yelled, "Get out! Scat!"

They watched the hole.

"I don't see anything," Holly whispered.

"Me either," Kat agreed.

They heard Mom pounding inside the house. "Out! Out! Out!" she hollered.

Something appeared at the hole. It was a black nose. It was two dark eyes. It was two little ears.

"I see it!" Holly shrieked.

The nose and eyes and ears went back in the hole. Kat held her hand over Holly's mouth. And the nose came back out again.

"I see it too. Be quiet," Kat whispered. She took her hand away.

Inside the house Mom hollered and pounded. And outside the animal popped out of the hole. It was not a mouse. It was furry and brown. Kat saw the bushy tail. It was a squirrel!

Kat and Holly watched the squirrel. In one leap it swung onto the tree next to the house. Then it leaped onto the roof and scampered away.

"Hoorah!" Kat shouted.

Holly grabbed Kat's arm. "Kat! Look!" she whispered.

Another nose poked out of the hole. Black eyes. Little ears. Another squirrel popped out, jumped onto the tree and leaped onto the roof.

"Mom! Mom! Two squirrels!" Kat yelled.

She and Holly started towards the house. Then they stopped. Another squirrel was at the hole. They watched it pop out. It scampered *down* the tree and ran across the yard.

"Mom! Mom!" Holly shrieked.

Mom came to the bedroom window and leaned out. "Two squirrels! Imagine that!" She held Putter by the collar to keep him from jumping out.

"Three!" Holly laughed. "There were three!"

9
Silence

Mom came out of the house with Putter at her heels. "Three squirrels! No wonder there was so much racket in the attic!"

She climbed up the ladder and studied the hole. "I have to patch the hole," she said.

In the garage Mom found scraps of wood and a box of nails. Putter raced behind her with his nose to the ground. Back on the ladder, Mom nailed a wood scrap over the hole. Then she put the old piece of siding on top of it.

"Won't they get back in?" Kat asked. "Won't they chew another hole?"

"No way," Mom said. "They got in under the loose siding. Now the siding will stay in place." She nailed another scrap of wood across the siding. Then she climbed down and looked up at her work.

"It looks funny," Holly said.

Kat poked her in the arm. "It looks—strong," she said.

"It's just temporary," Mom said. "I'll order a new piece of siding and put it on."

Kat turned to Holly. "It will be good as new. You'll see."

"No more squirrels," Holly said.

Mom hugged her.

In the house Mom fried bacon. Then she made waffles with blueberries. Blueberry waffles were Kat's favorite breakfast. Holly liked them too. Mom made a waffle for Putter—without the blueberries.

"Good old Putter," Mom said.

In the middle of the night, Kat heard Putter bark. But there was no *clickety click thump*. There was no *nibby nibby crunch*.

Kat stared at the ceiling. It seemed strange. The squirrels were gone. Kat was glad the squirrels did not catch their tails in the mousetraps. She was glad they were not exterminated and had not suffocated. But she was glad they were not in her attic. She went back to sleep.

"Time to get up!" Mom called. "It's almost nine!"

Kat jumped out of bed and woke up Holly. Dad always came at ten o'clock sharp.

Kat and Holly dressed in their good clothes. Maybe Dad would take them to the zoo today.

Mom was in the kitchen. "Did you sleep well?" she asked. "Any monsters?"

Kat and Holly shook their heads.

Just then Kat heard Dad's car in the driveway.

"Daddy!" Holly shrieked. They both ran for their coats.

"Don't forget your hats," Mom said. "It isn't spring yet."

Holly ran out of the house without looking back. "Daddy!" she hollered as she ran to the car.

Dad got out and scooped Holly into his arms. Kat took both hats and hurried out.

"Daddy! Guess what!" Holly was saying. "There were squirrels in our attic! Three of them!"

"Three squirrels? In the attic?" Dad said. He put Holly down and hugged Kat close. "Were you afraid? What did you do?"

"Holly was afraid there was a monster," Kat said.

Holly clung to Dad's coat sleeve. "Only a *little* afraid."

"So what did you do?" Dad asked Kat. "Did you get them out?"

Just then Putter barked, and Kat looked back. At the door Putter stood on his hind legs. Mom waved.

"We got them out, Dad," Kat said. "We got them out alive!"

"Good for you!" Dad said. He scooped Holly up in his arms again.

Kat stood beside them, smiling. Good for us, she thought. Good for us!

Put a picture of your dog
in this box

D1316950

Your Dog's Name

Your Dog's License Number _____

Date of Birth _____

Your Dog's Veterinarian _____

Address _____

Phone Number _____

Medications _____

Vet Emergency Number _____

Additional Emergency Numbers _____

Feeding Instructions _____

Exercise Routine _____

Favorite Treats _____

Tear me out!

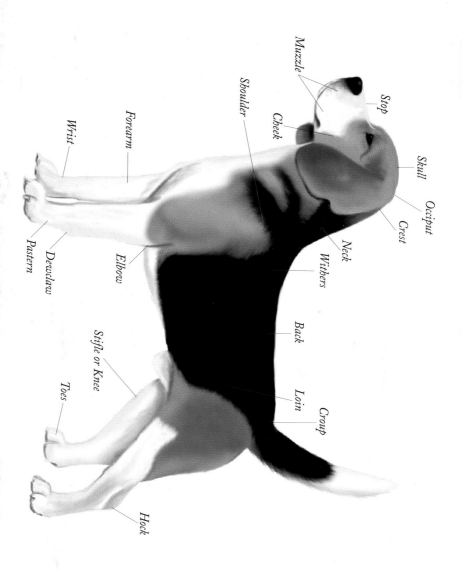

Muzzle

Stop

Skull

Occiput

Crest

Neck

Withers

Back

Loin

Croup

Hock

Toes

Stifle or Knee

Pastern

Dewclaw

Elbow

Wrist

Forearm

Shoulder

Cheek

Meet the Beagle

Beagles are scent-hounds that were originally bred to hunt European hares.

The Beagle is known as a miniature Foxhound and a cousin of the Basset Hound.

Beagles live and work in packs, which is why they are so friendly, co-operative and devoted.

Beagles like to bark. During the hunt, their voices let their masters know where they are and how they're doing.

There are two types of Beagles—those under 13 inches high and those over 13 inches high.

Very little grooming is required to keep a Beagle looking clean and healthy.

Beagles enjoy the great out-doors and should go for several walks a day.

The overall temperament of the Beagle is bold and friendly, not too wary of strangers, but not too overbearing either.

Beagles have hearty appetites and are not as picky about their food as other small dogs.

The most famous Beagle of all is Snoopy.

Consulting Editor

AN DUNBAR PH.D., MRCVS

Featuring Photographs by

WINTER CHURCHILL

PHOTOGRAPHY

Howell Book House

A Simon & Schuster Macmillan Company
633 Broadway
New York, NY 10019

Macmillan Publishing books may be purchased
or business or sales promotional use. For information please write: Special Markets
Department, Macmillan Publishing USA,
633 Broadway, New York, NY 10019.

Library of Congress Cataloging-in-Publication
Data
The essential beagle.
            p. cm.
    Includes bibliographical references (p. 87) and
index.
    ISBN 1-58245-019-6
    1. Beagle (Dog Breed) I. Howell Book House.
    SF429.B3E77   1999
                             98-46321
    636.753'7—dc21   CIP

Manufactured in the United States of America
0 9 8 7 6 5 4 3 2 1

Series Director: Michele Matrisciani
Production Team: Linda Quigley, Terri Sheehan,
    Donna Wright
Book Design: Paul Costello
Photography courtesy of Diane Robinson: 75, 78, 79
All other photos by Winter Churchill Photography.

ARE YOU READY?!

☐ Have you prepared your home and your family for your new pet?

☐ Have you gotten the proper supplies you'll need to care for your dog?

☐ Have you found a veterinarian that you (and your dog) are comfortable with?

☐ Have you thought about how you want your dog to behave?

☐ Have you arranged your sched-ule to accommodate your dog's needs for exercise and attention?

No matter what stage you're at with your dog—still thinking about get-ting one, or he's already part of the family—this Essential guide will provide you with the practical infor-mation you need to understand and care for your canine companion. Of course you're ready—you have this book!

Beagle

SIGHT

Beagles can detect movement at a greater distance than we can, but they can't see as well up close. They can also see better in less light, but can't distinguish many colors.

SOUND

Beagles can hear about four times better than we can, and they can hear high-pitched sounds especially well.

SMELL

A Beagle's nose is his greatest sensory organ. A dog's sense of smell is so great he can follow a trail that's weeks old. Because the Beagle is a scent-hound, his nose is usually on the ground and his sense of smell is especially on track. In fact, Beagles are often recruited into the Beagle Brigade, a group of Beagles used by the U.S. Customs department, to sniff out drugs and food being smuggled in and out of the country.

TASTE

Beagles have fewer taste buds than we do, so they're likelier to try anything—and usually do, which is why it's important for their owners to monitor their food intake. Dogs are omnivorous, which means they eat meat as well as vegetables.

TOUCH

Beagles are social animals and love to be petted, groomed and played with.

CHAPTER ONE

Getting to Know Your Beagle

The Beagle is a hound, a member of a select fraternity within the canine world, bred for centuries to hunt as part of a large pack. He is the little cousin of the Foxhound so often depicted in the numerous paintings of horses and hounds in the English countryside. He is the more active, less melancholic cousin of the Basset Hound, and, like the Basset, his primary quarry is the hare or rabbit.

New owners of a Beagle puppy may find it amusing that the tiny creature cruises around the house with his nose to the ground; this is both a legacy from his pack-hunting ancestors and a rehearsal for future hunting if allowed the opportunity. It can safely be said that the Beagle experiences much of the world through his nose. Within days of settling into his new home, a Beagle will have memorized a rather detailed olfactory map of his territory, and his "rounds" each day will tell him whether anyone new has been around.

The Beagle experiences much of the world through his nose.

A Gregarious Fellow

Remember, the Beagle has been bred to live as a member of a *pack*. While our modern Beagle may be a member of a pack consisting of himself and your family, his temperament is predictably excellent (assuming, of course, he is well treated), and his loyalty, courage and devotion have remained unchanged over the centuries.

Vocalization and Other "Hound Habits"

The Beagle is possessed of a very musical voice, and while not "yappy," the Beagle can be quite vocal in expressing himself, especially if a

stray dog or cat enters his territory. This characteristic has led many people to praise the Beagle's usefulness as a watchdog.

The downside to all this hound heritage is a tendency sometimes to be a bit headstrong, and cases of selective hearing in Beagles is not uncommon. If a Beagle is following a trail or just sniffing something really interesting, he will not be as likely to respond as if he were in the house—he is hearing "inner voices"! A knowledgeable Beagle owner will plan for these contingencies as part of his ongoing training.

Another "hound habit" is rolling in foul-smelling matter. While many breeds do this, it seems that Beagles, again because of their good noses, find more of it to roll in. Often they are just as inclined to eat such things! Such an event is no big deal, but for a house pet it usually means an unscheduled bath.

YOUR BEAGLE'S ATTITUDE

There is a fairly wide range of temperament in today's Beagle. Beagles bred for show, on average, tend to be bolder than their field-bred counterparts. On the face of it, this seems counterintuitive, since one thinks of "hunting dogs" as bold, or even aggressive, but many superb hunting Beagles are quite shy. A shy show Beagle, on the other hand, would never stand a chance in the ring if he were constantly worried about the presence of strangers, especially when one of them is the judge. Obviously, what we want is a bold, friendly little hound not too wary of strangers, but not too overbearing either.

This story will take you into the inner workings of the Beagle.

DAISY, THE TYPICAL BEAGLE

Daisy half wakes up and yawns on the couch where she has been curled up most of the afternoon. At almost 3 years old, she never causes any

Your Beagle should be bold and outgoing, but not overbearing.

3

major problems around the house; her puppy teething ended when she was about a year old, she was well housebroken by 6 months old, she never has accidents and she no longer feels upset being left alone when her people are at work.

Some days they leave her outdoors in the fenced backyard, where she has a house she can retreat into if it starts to rain, but now it is early spring, and the yard is wet and muddy. She is concerned that there may be something wrong with her people: They are always wiping her feet if she is muddy, and on those occasions when she is lucky enough to find something really mellow to roll in, they act like she has done something awful and give her a bath.

She is getting progressively wakeful as the hour when her people generally return approaches. More cars are driving by, and suddenly one is approaching that she recognizes by its sound. She is waiting at the kitchen door as the car door slams, and the footsteps tell her it is her master. He comes in and doesn't notice her wagging her tail enthusiastically. His jacket is off, his necktie is askew and he is shuffling a stack of mail.

Beagles need plenty of attention and quality time with their people.

Getting His Attention

Not used to being ignored quite this much, she lightly rests her front paws on his leg and looks up expectantly. She was discouraged from "jumping up" as a puppy, but somehow she is allowed to do this. Now she has his attention, as he bends down to stroke her under the chin, and follows up with an ear rub. "How was your day, Daisy? Busy protecting the homestead, or were you dreaming of rabbits all day?"

At the mention of the "R Word," her excitement level climbs, and instantly he realizes what he has done. That word, along with "biscuit," "treat" and her name all get predictable responses. He knows she would love to go for a run, and hasn't had much fun lately. He changes into jeans, and returns to the kitchen with her leash in hand. "So, do you want to chase a rabbit?" She begins squirming so from excitement that he has difficulty attaching the leash!

Time for Rabbits!

Only a couple of blocks away is a small woodlot. It is early spring, approaching dusk, and, predictably, there is a cottontail rabbit nibbling the clover at the edge of the woods.

Daisy does not see it, but her master, because of his height, does.

He lets her off the leash, and she bounds off towards the woods, her tail up and practically vibrating with excitement. Soon she drifts over to where the cottontail was dining, and her whole body begins to wag! Her tail is whipping from side to side as she begins to whimper slightly, then breaks out into a Beagle aria!

Soon she is trotting along the line of scent left behind by the rabbit and singing her heart out with each track. A couple of kids interrupt their baseball game to investigate the commotion. "Hey, Mister, what's wrong with your dog?" asks one with great concern.

"She is chasing a rabbit," he explains, and then answers the inevitable questions about whether she sees the rabbit (no), whether she will catch the rabbit (no, the rabbit will go into a hole if it gets too worried), whether she bites (no) and so on. All the while he is standing in one place and keeping track of the "hunt" by ear, only occasionally catching a glimpse of her in the woods. Sud-denly the rabbit pops out of the cover and darts back into the woods.

Still Sniffing

A minute later, Daisy is in the open field, quiet now because the sudden change in terrain and change in direction have temporarily baffled her. Her nose is virtually vacuuming the short grass at the edge of the field when she finds the track and lifts her head in a long, musical note. The rabbit has completed one full circuit of its territory, and Daisy has successfully solved all its attempts to throw her off the trail. Before she can pursue it back into the woods, her master snaps her leash back on and praises her.

Back home, her master checks her thoroughly for ticks, then

Your Beagle's healthy appetite should be offset by plenty of exercise.

5

A DOG'S SENSES

Sight: Dogs can't see as well up close. They can also see better in less light, but can't distinguish many colors.

Sound: Dogs can hear about four times better than we can, and they can hear high-pitched sounds especially well. They have a wide range of vocalizations, including barks, whimpers, moans and whines.

Smell: A dog's nose is his greatest sensory organ. His sense of smell is so great he can follow a trail that's weeks old, detect odors diluted to one-millionth the concentration we'd need to notice them, even sniff out a person under water!

Taste: Dogs have fewer taste buds than we do, so they're likelier to try anything—and usually do, which is why it's especially important for their owners to monitor their food intake. Dogs are omnivores, which means they eat meat as well as vegetable matter like grasses and weeds.

Touch: Dogs are social animals and love to be petted, groomed and played with.

himself as well. Back in the kitchen as he prepares dinner, Daisy sits hopefully at his feet waiting for either a spill or a lapse in judgment. Her people have been warned by the vet that she needs to watch her weight, especially now that she has been spayed. Her attentiveness has not been lost on him, and he asks whether she would like a treat.

ANYTHING FOR A TREAT

It sometimes amazes her that her people persist in asking such obvious questions, but she wags her tail, makes a halfhearted attempt at begging and follows him to the cookie jar, where he extracts a small biscuit and tosses it to her. Her catch is flawless, as usual, and she retreats to her sanctuary under the kitchen table to savor this prize. Unknown to her, her master makes a mental note to adjust her next feeding to allow for this in-between-meal snack! He also makes a note to get her out running more often; it would keep both of them in better shape, especially if he ran along behind her, and besides, it is a perfect antidote for the stress of everyday modern life.

While the story of Daisy is a composite, it illustrates several things about the "soul" of a Beagle: They *love* to hunt, they are bonded to their packmates, (be they human or canine), they have a simple *joie de vivre* that all of us could well emulate and they love to eat.

In short, the Beagle has a rather simple world view. He is a hedonist (in the best sense of the word), a sportsman and a great proponent of "family values." What more could one want in a Best Friend?

CHARACTERISTICS OF THE BEAGLE

Experiences the world through his nose

A family vs. a one-person dog

Likes to use his voice

Can be headstrong

Likes to explore

Doesn't need excessive exercise

CHAPTER TWO

Homecoming

Before bringing home your new family member, a little planning can help make the transition easier. The first decision to make is where the puppy will live. Will she have access to the entire house or be limited to certain rooms? A similar consideration applies to the yard. It is simpler to control a puppy's activities and to housetrain the puppy if she is confined to definite areas. If doors do not exist where needed, baby gates make satisfactory temporary barriers.

A dog crate is an excellent investment and is an invaluable aid in raising a puppy. It provides a safe, quiet place where a dog can sleep. Used properly, a crate helps with housetraining. The same crate can be used when traveling. A crate that will fit an adult Beagle is approximately 24 inches wide, 36 inches deep and 26 inches high.

PUPPY-PROOFING

Before the puppy comes home, examine your household as if you were "baby-proofing." Even though you will not likely give your puppy free rein of the house, it is best to guard your valuables against the teething puppy, and remove anything from her reach that may be injurious or toxic. Anything small enough to be swallowed or that can be chewed or shredded until small enough to be swallowed needs to be removed.

Similarly, many common house-plants are toxic to dogs and cats, so keep them out of reach. Sprays can be applied to furniture items that will make them taste bad and therefore discourage chewing, but if you have something you especially value, keep it well hidden. Also, remember that electrical cords, when chewed, can prove fatal.

USING A CRATE

Most trainers today advocate the use of the crate as a way of housetraining a new puppy. An added advantage is that the crate can later be used for travel or for those occasions when you wish the puppy to be in protective custody, like when little children are visiting. The principle, as it applies to housetraining, is that puppies are reluctant to eliminate where they sleep.

9

Puppy-proofing your home protects your Beagle from injury and keeps your personal items from becoming chew toys.

PUPPY ESSENTIALS

To prepare yourself and your family for your puppy's homecoming, and to be sure your pup has what she needs, you should obtain the following:

Food and Water Bowls: One for each. We recommend stainless steel or heavy crockery—something solid but easy to clean.

Collar: An adjustable buckle collar is best. Remember, your pup's going to grow fast!

Leash: Style is nice, but durability and your comfort while holding it count, too. You can't go wrong with leather for most dogs.

I.D. Tag: Inscribed with your name and phone number.

Bed and/or Crate Pad: Something soft, washable and big enough for your soon-to-be-adult dog.

Crate: Make housetraining easier and provide a safe, secure den for your dog with a crate—it only looks like a cage to you!

Toys: As much fun to buy as they are for your pup to play with. Don't overwhelm your puppy with too many toys, though, especially the first few days she's home. And be sure to include something hollow you can stuff with goodies, like a Kong.

Grooming Supplies: The proper brushes, special shampoo, toenail clippers, a toothbrush and doggy toothpaste.

By the time your puppy is weaned, she will probably be eating three times a day. It is common for young puppies to eliminate after every meal, as well as after waking. Knowing this makes it possible, with some planning and keen observation, to anticipate your puppy's need to use the outdoors or newspaper, depending on which venue you choose.

The crate must be only as large as you absolutely need it to be, based on the anticipated size of your Beagle at maturity. If the crate is too large, the puppy will convert it into a two-room suite, making one part the bedroom and the other part the bathroom.

Don't feel bad about keeping your puppy in the crate for reasonable periods of time. Most people do not realize that young puppies, like babies, sleep a good deal of the time. After relatively brief periods of training or play, your puppy will soon look forward to the security her crate affords.

COLLARS, LEASHES AND OTHER SUPPLIES

You will want to have a collar and leash ready before you pick up your

A dog crate provides your Beagle with a safe place to relax—this guy's enjoying the view from on top before settling inside his crate.

puppy, but don't expect to use them much right away. The more gradually things happen, the less stressful on both of you. Consequently, it is best to get the puppy acclimated to the collar (a lightweight nylon type is best for this stage) before using the leash.

The first encounter with the leash can be traumatic sometimes, and some trainers recommend letting the dog get used to the feel of both collar and leash before attempting a walk. Lightweight and inexpensive are the keys here, as your Beagle will soon outgrow these puppy trappings.

Get your Beagle used to the feel of a lightweight collar and leash before trying to walk her.

Your Beagle will need spill-proof bowls for her food and water.

BOWLS, BEDS AND TOYS

Similarly, when you consider such possessions as feeding bowls, beds and toys, keep in mind that what is appropriate for a mature Beagle may not be for a young puppy. A puppy's food and water bowls are better if they are more shallow than ones used for older animals, and while the puppy's bed is often an old rug or towel, you might prefer (once the accidents cease) something filled with an aromatic stuffing like cedar shavings, which will not only help keep her sweet-smelling

but are reputed to help control fleas.

The adult feeding bowls should be large enough for a full day's feed and water; beyond that, you are on your own as far as style and material. Try to think somewhat practically, however, and remember that your Beagle can't read or see colors. Spill-proof is always a good option, especially for the water bowl, but dishwasher-proof is more important. Whereas it was always prescribed that bowls be regularly disinfected, today's high-temperature dishwashers make it feasible to wash your Beagle's dishes along with everyone else's.

Your puppy will need to chew for much longer than you would like; chew toys are an acceptable alternative to your antiques. Ask your vet about what is both satisfying and safe for your pup. Toys made of rawhide or other organic matter are degradable and therefore can be ingested. Basically, all you want your puppy to swallow is her food, so be careful not to accidentally harm your puppy with these treats. As your puppy gets bigger and her digestive system matures, these things may come off the forbidden list, but, again, check with your vet.

OUTDOOR TIME

The Beagle does not require a great deal of exercise, and this is especially true of little puppies. However, if you would like to institute a regimen involving walks, or, later, the occasional rabbit chase, try to be as consistent and regular as possible. If you are lucky enough to have a fenced yard, a bench or doghouse with a flat roof will give your older puppy a chance to jump up and, in the process, change her perspective on things. It will also give her a dry spot in which to sun herself when the ground may be damp or too cool to make her nap as restful as it could be.

Once your puppy is close to her mature size (approximately 6 to 8 months of age), you will want to replace the puppy collar, lead and feeding bowls with something more age appropriate. Some Beagle owners prefer the traditional leather to the newer nylon items, but either type works well.

DON'T FORGET I.D.

Some supply houses offer free nameplates on both collars and leads. The mandatory dog license from your municipality is not sufficient to

IDENTIFY YOUR DOG

It is a terrible thing to think about, but your dog could somehow, someday, get lost or stolen. For safety's sake, every dog should wear a buckle collar with an identification tag. A tag is the first thing a stranger will look for on a lost dog. Inscribe the tag with your name and phone number.

There are two ways to permanently identify your dog. The first is a tattoo, placed on the inside of your dog's thigh. The tattoo should be your social security number or your dog's AKC registration number. The second is a microchip, a rice-sized pellet that is inserted under the dog's skin at the base of the neck, between the shoulder blades. When a scanner is passed over the dog, it will beep, notifying the person that the dog has a chip. The scanner will then show a code, identifying the dog.

13

guarantee your pet's safe return in the event she strays from home, but a nameplate secured to the collar with your name, address and phone number will help. Many people add "collect" or "reward" to the tag to encourage people to do the right thing.

Only after you have secured these things for your puppy, as well

HOUSEHOLD DANGERS

Curious puppies and inquisitive dogs get into trouble not because they are bad, but simply because they want to investigate the world around them. It's our job to protect our dogs from harmful substances, like the following:

In the House

cleaners, especially pine oil

perfumes, colognes, aftershaves

medications, vitamins

office and craft supplies

electric cords

chicken or turkey bones

chocolate, onions

some house and garden plants, like ivy, oleander and poinsettia

In the Garage

antifreeze

garden supplies, like snail and slug bait, pesticides, fertilizers, mouse and rat poisons

as the kind of food recommended by the breeder, are you ready to bring your new puppy home. It is best to do this at the beginning of a weekend or vacation, if possible, when you can spend some time bonding and getting to know each other. And, incidentally, don't expect a lot of sleep the first night or two.

CHAPTER THREE

To Good Health

The strongest body and soundest genetic background will not help a dog lead a healthy life unless he receives regular attention from his owner. Dogs are susceptible to infection, parasites and diseases for which they have no natural immunity. It is up to us to take preventive measures to make sure that none of these interfere with our dog's health. It may help to think of the upkeep of a dog's health in relation to the calendar. Certain things need to be done on a weekly, monthly and annual basis.

PREVENTIVE HEALTH CARE

Weekly grooming can be the single best monitor of a dog's overall health.

The actual condition of the coat and skin and the "feel" of the body can indicate good health or potential problems. Grooming will help you discover small lumps on or under the skin in the early stages before they become large enough to be seen without close examination.

You may spot fleas and ticks when brushing the coat and examining the skin. Besides harboring diseases and parasites, they can make daily life a

Run your hands regularly over your dog to feel for any injuries.

Flea Control

Flea control is never a simple endeavor. Dogs bring fleas inside, where they lay eggs in the carpeting and furniture—anywhere your dog goes in the house. Consequently, real control is a matter of not only treating the dog but also the other environments the flea inhabits. The yard can be sprayed, and in the house, sprays and flea bombs can be used, but there are more choices for the dog. Flea sprays are effective for one to two weeks. Dips applied to the dog's coat following a bath have equal periods of effectiveness. The disadvantage of both of these

nightmare for some dogs. Some Beagles are allergic to even a couple of fleas on their bodies. They scratch, chew and destroy their coat and skin because of fleas.

Puppies and dogs that spend a lot of time outdoors will need to be checked for ticks and fleas.

is that some dogs may have problems with the chemicals.

Flea collars prevent the fleas from traveling to your dog's head, where it's moister and more hospitable. Dog owners tend to leave flea collars on their dogs long after they've ceased to be effective. Again, some dogs may have problems with flea collars, and children should never be allowed to handle them.

Some owners opt for a product that works from the inside out. One such option is a pill (prescribed by a veterinarian) that you give to the dog on a regular basis. The chemicals in the pill course through the dog's bloodstream, and when a flea bites, the blood kills the flea.

Another available option is a product that comes in capsule form. The liquid in the capsule is applied near the dog's shoulders, close to the skin where it distributes into the skin and coat to protect against fleas and ticks. Ask your veterinarian about this nontoxic, long-lasting tick and flea preventative.

Ticks

As you examine your dog, check also for ticks that may have lodged in his skin, particularly around the ears or

Use tweezers to remove ticks from your dog.

in the hair at the base of the ear, the armpits or around the inguinal region. If you find a tick, which is a small insect about the size of a pencil eraser when engorged with blood,

FLEAS AND TICKS

There are so many safe, effective products available now to combat fleas and ticks that—thankfully—they are less of a problem. Prevention is key, however. Ask your veterinarian about starting your puppy on a flea/tick repellant right away. With this, regular grooming and monitoring your puppy's skin and coat, your dog and your home should stay pest-free. Without this attention, you risk infesting your dog and your home, and you're in for an ugly and costly battle to clear up the problem.

smear it with petroleum jelly. As the tick suffocates, it will back out and you can then grab it with tweezers and kill it. If the tick doesn't back out, grab it with tweezers and gently pull it out, twisting very gently. Don't just grab and pull or the tick's head may remain in the skin, causing an infection or abscess for which veterinary treatment may be required.

A word of caution: Don't use your fingers or fingernails to pull out ticks. Ticks can carry a number of diseases, including Lyme disease, Rocky Mountain spotted fever and others, all of which can be very serious.

Proper Ear Care

Another weekly job is cleaning the ears. Many times an ear problem is evident if a dog scratches his ears or shakes his head frequently. Clean ears are less likely to develop problems, and if something does occur, it will be spotted while it can be treated easily. If a dog's ears are very dirty and seem to need cleaning on a daily basis, it is a good indication that something else is going on in the ears besides ordinary dirt and the normal accumulation of earwax. A visit to the veterinarian may indicate a situation that needs special attention.

Brushing Teeth

Regular brushing of the teeth often does not seem necessary when a dog is young and spends much of his time chewing; the teeth always seem to be immaculately clean. As a dog ages, it becomes more important to brush the teeth daily.

To help prolong the health of your dog's mouth, he should have his teeth cleaned twice a year at a veterinary clinic. Observing the mouth regularly, checking for the formation of abnormalities or broken teeth, can lead to early detection or oral cancer or infection.

Keeping Nails Trimmed

The nails on all feet should be kept short enough so they do not touch the ground when the dog walks.

Check your dog's teeth frequently and brush them regularly.

18

Dogs with long nails can have difficulty walking on hard or slick surfaces. This can be especially true of older dogs. As nails grow longer, the only way the foot can compensate and retain balance is for the toes themselves to spread apart, causing the foot itself to become flattened and splayed.

Keeping Eyes Clear

A Beagle's eyes rarely need special attention. A small amount of matter in the corner of the eye is normal, as is a bit of "tearing." Beagles with eyelashes that turn inward and rub against the eye itself often exhibit more tearing than normal due to the irritation to the eyes. These eyelashes can be surgically removed if it appears to be a problem, but are often ignored.

Excessive tearing can be an indication that a tear duct is blocked. This, too, can be corrected by a simple surgical procedure. Eye discharge that is thicker and mucous-like in consistency is often a sign of some type of eye infection or actual injury to the eye. This can be verified by a veterinarian, who will provide a topical ointment to place in the corner of the eye. Most minor eye injuries heal quickly if proper action is taken.

VACCINES

Your puppy's breeder started him on a vaccination schedule that you will need to maintain.

Since the mid-1970s, parvovirus and coronavirus have been the cause of death for thousands of dogs. Puppies and older dogs are most frequently affected by these illnesses. Fortunately, vaccines for these are now routinely given on a yearly basis in combination with the DHL shot—the combined shot is referred to as DHLPP.

Kennel cough, though rarely dangerous in a healthy dog that receives

YOUR PUPPY'S VACCINES

Vaccines are given to prevent your dog from getting an infectious disease like canine distemper or rabies. Vaccines are the ultimate preventive medicine. That's why it is necessary for your dog to be vaccinated routinely. Puppy vaccines start at 8 weeks of age for the five-in-one DHLPP vaccine. Your veterinarian will put your puppy on a proper schedule and should remind you when to bring in your dog for shots.

of the body is commonly inhabited by a variety of parasites. Most of these are in the worm family. Tapeworms, roundworms, whipworms, hookworms and heartworm all plague dogs. There are also several types of protozoa, mainly *coccidia* and *giardia*, that cause problems.

The common tapeworm is acquired by the dog eating infected fleas or lice. Normally one is not aware that a healthy dog even has tapeworms. The only clues may be a dull coat, a loss of weight despite a good appetite or occasional gastrointestinal problems. Confirmation is by the presence of worm segments in the stool. These appear as small, pinkish-white, flattened rectangular-shaped pieces. When dry, they look like rice. If segments are not present, diagnosis can be made by the discovery of eggs when a stool sample is examined under a microscope. Ridding a dog temporarily of tapeworm is easy with a worming medicine prescribed by a veterinarian. Over-the-counter wormers are not effective for tapeworms and may be dangerous. Long-term tapeworm control is not possible unless the flea situation is also handled.

Ascarids are the most common roundworm (nematode) found in

Your puppy's breeder started him on a vaccination schedule that you will need to maintain.

proper treatment, can be annoying. It can be picked up anywhere that large numbers of dogs congregate, such as veterinary clinics, grooming shops, boarding kennels, obedience classes and dog shows. The Bordatella vaccine, given twice a year, will protect a dog from getting most strains of kennel cough. It is often not routinely given, so it may be necessary to request it.

INTERNAL PARASITES

While the exterior part of a dog's body hosts fleas and ticks, the inside dogs. Adult dogs that have round-worms rarely exhibit any symptoms that would indicate the worm is in their body. These worms are cylindrical in shape and may be as long as 4 to 5 inches. They do pose a real danger to puppies, where they are usually passed from the mother through the uterus to the unborn puppies.

It is wise to assume that all puppies have roundworms. In heavy infestations they will actually appear in the puppy stools, though their presence is best diagnosed by a stool sample. Treatment is easy and can begin as early as 2 weeks of age

Common internal parasites (l–r): roundworm, whipworm, tapeworm and hookworm.

and is administered every two weeks thereafter until eggs no longer appear in a stool sample or dead worms are not found in the stool following treatment. Severely infected puppies can die from roundworm infestation. Again, the worming medication should be obtained through a veterinarian.

Hookworm is usually found in warmer climates and infestation

21

Regular visits to the veterinarian and preventive care will help keep your Beagle healthy.

WHAT'S WRONG WITH MY DOG?

We've listed some common symptoms of health problems and their possible causes. If any of the following symptoms appear serious immediately or persist for more than 24 hours, make an appointment to see your veterinarian immediately.

CONDITIONS	POSSIBLE CAUSES
DIARRHEA	Intestinal upset, typically caused by eating something bad or over-eating. Can also be a viral infection, a bad case of nerves or anxiety or a parasite infection. If you see blood in the feces, get to the vet right away.
VOMITING/RETCHING	Dogs regurgitate fairly regularly (bitches for their young), whenever something upsets their stomach, or even out of excitement or anxiety. Often dogs eat grass, which, because it's indigestible in its pure form, irritates their stomachs and causes them to vomit. Getting a good look at *what* your dog vomited can better indicate what's causing it.
COUGHING	Obstruction in the throat; virus (kennel cough); roundworm infestation; congestive heart failure.
RUNNY NOSE	Because dogs don't catch colds like people, a runny nose is a sign of congestion or irritation.
LOSS OF APPETITE	Because most dogs are hearty and regular eaters, a loss of appetite can be your first and most accurate sign of a serious problem.
LOSS OF ENERGY (LETHARGY)	Any number of things could be slowing down your dog, from an infection to internal tumors to overexercise—even overeating.

is generally from ingestion of larvae from the ground or penetration of the skin by larvae. Hookworms can cause anemia, diarrhea and emaciation. As these worms are very tiny and not visible to the eye, their diagnosis must be made by a veterinarian.

Whipworms live in the large intestine and cause few if any

CONDITIONS	POSSIBLE CAUSES
STINKY BREATH	Imagine if you never brushed your teeth! Foul-smelling breath indicates plaque and tartar buildup that could possibly have caused infection. Start brushing your dog's teeth.
LIMPING	This could be caused by something as simple as a hurt or bruised pad, to something as complicated as hip dysplasia, torn ligaments or broken bones.
CONSTANT ITCHING	Probably due to fleas, mites or an allergic reaction to food or environment (your vet will need to help you determine what your dog's allergic to).
RED, INFLAMED ITCHY SPOTS	Often referred to as "hot spots," these are particularly common on coated breeds. They're caused by a bacterial infection that gets aggravated as the dog licks and bites at the spot.
BALD SPOTS	These are the result of excessive itching or biting at the skin so that the hair follicles are damaged; excessively dry skin; mange; calluses; and even infections. You need to determine what the underlying cause is.
STINKY EARS/HEADSHAKING	Take a look under your dog's ear flap. Do you see brown, waxy buildup? Clean the ears with something soft and a special cleaner, and don't use cotton swabs or go too deep into the ear canal.
UNUSUAL LUMPS	Could be fatty tissue, could be something serious (infection, trauma, tumor). Don't wait to find out.

23

symptoms. Dogs usually become infected when they ingest larvae in contaminated soil. Again, diagnosis and treatment should all be done by a veterinarian. One of the easiest ways to control these parasites is by picking up stools on a daily basis. This will help prevent the soil from becoming infested.

The protozoa can be trickier to diagnose and treat. Coccidiosis and giardia are the most common, and primarily affect young puppies. They are generally associated with overcrowded, unsanitary conditions and can be acquired from the mother (if she is a carrier), the premises themselves (soil) or even water, especially rural puddles and streams.

The most common symptom of protozoan infection is mucous-like, blood-tinged feces. It is only with freshly collected samples that diagnosis of this condition can be made. With *coccidiosis,* besides diarrhea, the puppies will appear listless and lose their appetites. Puppies often harbor the protozoa and show no symptoms unless placed under stress. Consequently, many times a puppy will not become ill until he goes to his new home. Once diagnosed, treatment is quick and effective and the puppy returns to normal almost immediately.

Heartworm

The most serious of the common internal parasites is the heartworm. A dog that is bitten by a mosquito infected with the heartworm microfilaria (larvae) will develop worms that are 6 to 12 inches long. As these worms mature they take up residence in the dog's heart.

The symptoms of heartworm may include coughing, tiring easily, difficulty breathing and weight loss. Heart failure and liver disease may eventually result. Verification of heartworm infection is done by drawing blood and screening for the microfilaria.

In areas where heartworm is a risk, it is best to place a dog on a preventative, usually a pill given once a month.

At least once a year a dog should have a full veterinary examination. The overall condition of the dog can be observed and a blood sample collected for a complete yearly screening. This way the dog's thyroid function can be tested and the job the dog's organs are doing can be monitored. If there are any problems, this form of testing can spot trouble areas while they are easily treatable.

Proper care, regular vaccinations, periodic stool checks and preventative medications for such things as heartworm will all help ensure your dog's health.

SPAYING/NEUTERING

Spaying a female dog or neutering a male is another way to make sure they lead long and healthy lives. Females spayed at a young age have almost no risk of developing mammary tumors or reproductive problems. Neutering a male is an excellent solution to dog aggression and also removes the chances of testicular cancer.

Female Beagles usually experience their first heat cycle somewhere between 6 months and 1 year of age. Unless spayed they will continue to come into heat on a regular cycle. The length of time between heats varies, with anything from every six months to a year being normal.

There is absolutely no benefit to a female having a first season before being spayed, nor in letting her have a litter. The decision to breed any dog should never be taken lightly. The obvious considerations are whether he or she is a good physical specimen of the breed and has a sound temperament. There are several genetic problems that are common to Beagles, such as molera, hydrocephalus, subluxation of the patella, heart murmur, cleft palate and hypoglycemia. Responsible breeders screen for these prior to making breeding decisions.

Finding suitable homes for puppies is another serious consideration. Due to their popularity, many people are attracted to Beagles and seek puppies without realizing the drawbacks of the breed.

ADVANTAGE OF SPAYING/NEUTERING

The greatest advantage of spaying (for females) or neutering (for males) your dog is that you are guaranteed that your dog will not produce puppies. There are too many puppies already available for too few homes. There are other advantages as well.

Advantages of Spaying

No messy heats.

No "suitors" howling at your windows or waiting in your yard.

No risk of pyometra (disease of the uterus) and decreases the incidence of mammary cancer.

Advantages of Neutering

Decreases incidents of fights, but doesn't affect the dog's personality.

Decreases roaming

Decreased incidences of urogenital diseases.

25

PREVENTIVE CARE PAYS

Using common sense, paying attention to your dog and working with your veterinarian, you can minimize health risks and problems. Use vet-recommended flea, tick and heartworm preventive medications; feed a nutritious diet appropriate for your dog's size, age and activity level; give your dog sufficient exercise and regular grooming; train and socialize your dog; keep current on your dog's shots; and enjoy all the years you have with your friend.

26

Owning a dog is a lifetime commitment to that animal. There are so many unwanted dogs—and yes, even unwanted Beagles—that people must be absolutely sure that they are not just adding to the pet overpopulation problem. When breeding a litter of puppies, it is more likely that you will lose more than you will make, when time, effort, equipment and veterinary costs are factored in.

COMMON PROBLEMS

Not Eating or Vomiting

One of the surest signs that a Beagle may be ill is if he does not eat. That is why it is important to know your dog's eating habits. For most dogs, one missed meal under normal conditions is not cause for alarm, but more than that and it is time to take your dog to the veterinarian to search for reasons. The vital signs should be checked and gums examined. Normally a dog's gums are pink; if ill, they will be pale and gray.

There are many reasons why dogs vomit, and many of them are not cause for alarm. You should be concerned, however, when your dog vomits frequently over the period of a day. If the vomiting is associated with diarrhea, elevated temperature and lethargy, the cause is most likely a virus. The dog should receive supportive veterinary treatment if recovery is to proceed quickly. Vomiting that is not associated with other symptoms is often an indication of an intestinal blockage. Rocks, toys and clothing will lodge in a dog's intestine, preventing the normal passage of digested foods and liquids.

If a blockage is suspected, the first thing to do is get an x-ray of the stomach and intestinal region. Sometimes objects will pass on their own, but usually surgical removal of the object is necessary.

Diarrhea

Diarrhea is characterized as very loose to watery stools that a dog has difficulty controlling. It can be caused by anything as simple as changing diet, eating too much food, eating rich human food or having internal parasites.

First try to locate the source of the problem and remove it from the dog's access. Immediate relief is usually available by giving the dog an intestinal relief medication such as Kaopectate or Pepto-Bismol. Use the same amount per weight as for humans. Take the dog off his food for a day to allow the intestines to rest, then feed meals of cooked rice with bland ingredients added. Gradually add the dog's regular food back into his diet.

If diarrhea is bloody or has a more offensive odor than might be expected and is combined with vomiting and fever, it is most likely a virus and requires immediate veterinary attention. If worms are suspected as the cause, a stool sample should be examined by a veterinarian and treatment to rid the dog of the parasite should follow when the dog is back to normal. If allergies are suspected, a series of tests can be given to find the cause. This is especially

Get to know your Beagle's eating habits—if he starts missing meals he may be ill.

likely, if after recovery and no other evidence of a cause exists, a dog returns to his former diet and the diarrhea recurs.

Dehydration

To test your dog for dehydration, take some skin between your thumb and forefinger and lift the skin upward gently. If the skin does not go back to its original position quickly, the Beagle may be suffering from dehydration. Consult your veterinarian immediately.

27

POISON ALERT

If your dog has ingested a potentially poisonous substance, waste no time. Call the National Animal Poison Control Center hot line:

(800) 548-2423 ($30 per case) or

(900) 680-0000 ($20 first five minutes;
$2.95 each additional minute)

Poisoning

Vomiting, breathing with difficulty, diarrhea, cries of pain and abnormal body or breath odor are all signs that your pet may have ingested some poisonous substance. Poisons can also be inhaled, absorbed through the skin or injected into the skin, as in the case of a snakebite. Poisons require professional help without delay!

Some of the many household substances harmful to your dog.

Heatstroke

Heatstroke can quickly lead to death. Never leave your dog in a car, even with the windows open, even on a cloudy day with the car under the shade of a tree. Heat builds up quickly; your dog could die in a matter of minutes. Do not leave your Beagle outside on a hot day, especially if no shade or water is provided.

Heatstroke symptoms include collapse, high fever, diarrhea, vomiting, excessive panting and grayish lips. If you notice these symptoms, you need to cool the animal immediately. Try to reduce the body temperature with towels soaked in cold water; massage the body and legs very gently. Fanning the dog may help. If the dog will drink cool water, let him. If he will not drink, wipe the inside of his mouth with cool water. Get the dog to the nearest veterinary hospital. Do not delay!

Bee Stings

Bee stings are painful and may cause an allergic reaction. Symptoms may be swelling around the bite and difficulty breathing. Severe allergic reaction could lead to death. If a stinger is present, remove it. Apply a cold compress to reduce swelling and itching and an anti-inflammatory ointment or cream medication. Seek medical help.

Applying abdominal thrusts can save a choking dog.

Choking

Puppies are curious creatures and will naturally chew anything they can get into their mouths, be it a bone, a twig, stones, tiny toys, string or any number of things. These can get caught in the teeth or, worse, lodged in the throat and may finally rest in the stomach or intestines. Symptoms may be drooling, pawing at the mouth, gagging, difficulty breathing, blue tongue or mouth, difficulty swallowing and bloody vomit. If the foreign object can be seen and you can remove it easily, do so. If you can't remove it yourself, use the Heimlich maneuver. Place your dog on his side and, using both hands palms down, apply quick thrusts to the abdomen, just below the dog's last rib. If your dog won't lie down, grasp either side of the end of the rib cage and squeeze in short thrusts. Make a sharp enough movement to cause the air in the lungs to force the object out. If the cause cannot be found or removed, then professional help is needed.

WHEN TO CALL THE VETERINARIAN

In any emergency situation, you should call your veterinarian immediately. Try to stay calm when you call, and give the vet or the assistant as much information as possible before you leave for the clinic. That way, the staff will be able to take immediate, specific action when you arrive. Emergencies include:

Burns

Shock

Dehydration

Abdominal pain

Unusual bleeding or deep wounds

Broken bones

Call your veterinarian if you suspect any health troubles.

Bleeding

For open wounds, try to stop the bleeding by applying pressure to the wound for five minutes using

29

a sterile bandage. If bleeding has not stopped after this time, continue the pressure. Do not remove the pad if it sticks to the wound because more serious injury could result. Just place a new sterile bandage over the first, and apply a little more pressure to stop the bleeding. This procedure will usually be successful. Take the dog to the medical center for treatment especially if the bleeding cannot be controlled rapidly.

If bleeding cannot be stopped with pressure, try pressing on the upper inside of the leg or tail bleeding, press on the underside of the tail at its base. Do not attempt to stop the bleeding with a tourniquet unless the bleeding is profuse and cannot be stopped any other way. A tourniquet must be tight, consequently, it cannot be left on for more than a couple of minutes because it will stop the circulation. It could be more dangerous than the bleeding!

Burns

Do not put creams or oils on a burn. Cool water can be used to carefully wash the burn area. Transport to the veterinary clinic immediately.

INHERITED DISEASES OF BEAGLES

As noted at the beginning of this chapter, there are few problems that are unique to Beagles as a breed, but some things afflict Beagles more than other breeds, and some conditions that may not affect the whole breed may occur in certain strains or families.

Epilepsy

Epilepsy is a case in point, and while not hereditary, strictly speaking, it does appear in some families more than in others. The degree of severity can range from the petit mal form, which may appear to be nothing more than the dog "spacing out" for a few minutes, to grand mal, which involves loss of muscular control, stiffening and convulsing. The latter, often terrifying to the owner, may last several minutes, during which time you are convinced your dog is going to die. The dog then acts subdued or disoriented for a few more minutes and then acts as if nothing ever happened.

Closely related is another condition in Beagles known as "running fits," which occur when the hound is hunting and suddenly runs off as if being chased by the devil himself! A number of theories have been posited concerning this condition, including internal parasites, nutritional deficiencies or low blood sugar, but it remains a mystery.

In the case of epilepsy, mild forms present no major problems for the average house pet, but the more serious forms will no doubt require medication, as in the case of human epilepsy. Needless to say, an epileptic animal should never be bred.

Cherry Eye

Cherry Eye, or the infection and swelling of the third eyelid, is common in Beagles and may be treated with a simple surgical procedure or may even respond to antibiotics. The condition looks a lot worse than it is, since the swelling and redness are prominent, but many animals don't seem to know there is any problem. This problem should be distinguished from conjunctivitis, excessive tear production, corneal abrasions or a more serious condition known as dry eyes.

Back or Disc Problems

Back or disc problems occur occasionally in Beagles, but a Beagle with correct conformation kept in fit condition will be far less likely to have problems than will a longbodied or swaybacked Beagle carrying excessive weight. Treatment varies in type and in degree of success, so selection of a sound puppy from correctly built parents is the best form of prevention. Breeders could go a long way towards eliminating this condition by breeding older, sound animals with no history of back problems, since it rarely occurs in younger animals. In some cases, rest followed by moderate exercise will be enough to bring relief, but in more severe cases antiinflammatory drugs or even surgery may be required.

Lameness

Lameness, or the tendency to carry one foot off the ground, can be the result of any number of things, but

Make a temporary splint by wrapping the leg in firm casing, then bandaging it.

31

it is best to start with the simplest causes first before panicking. If your hound has been afield, the most common culprit is an embedded thorn in the foot. It is often easiest to "feel" for these with your fingers, as there may be very little material sticking out. Minor lacerations usually don't require any treatment.

If the foot shows any redness or swelling, your Beagle may have an interdigital cyst and will require antibiotic therapy. If the foot is not the cause of the lameness, there could be a problem with the knee or stifle joint, or he may have bruised, twisted or otherwise made some part of the running gear tender. Since Beagles are perfectly capable of motoring along just fine on three limbs, they often don't seem too upset when carrying one foot up. If the condition persists, however, it should be checked out.

This condition is very different from the one in which the hound

Keeping your Beagle fit will help prevent back and disc problems.

suddenly develops a stiff gait or a hunched appearance. This may signify any number of things, none of them good, so a trip to the vet would be in order.

Lyme disease, disc problems and kidney and enteric disease may all start like this, so don't delay professional diagnosis and treatment.

TAKING YOUR BEAGLE'S TEMPERATURE

Learn to take your pet's temperature. An elevated or depressed temperature may spell the difference between your hound just being "off his feed" for a day or the presence of some infection, which could be best treated early.

Ask someone to restrain the front end of your hound while you focus your attention on the other end. Grasp the base of the tail firmly, and with the other hand carefully insert a well-lubricated (with petroleum jelly) rectal thermometer into the anus. Holding your pet in this fashion should keep him fairly well immobilized. Be sure the thermometer you use is strong enough for this purpose; human oral-type thermometers are too fragile. The

A FIRST-AID KIT

Keep a canine first-aid kit on hand for general care and emergencies. Check it periodically to make sure liquids haven't spilled or dried up, and replace medications and materials after they're used. Your kit should include:

- Activated charcoal tablets
- Adhesive tape (1 and 2 inches wide)
- Antibacterial ointment (for skin and eyes)
- Aspirin (buffered or enteric coated, not Ibuprofen or acetaminophen)
- Bandages: gauze rolls (1 and 2 inches wide) and dressing pads
- Cotton balls
- Diarrhea medicine
- Dosing syringe
- Hydrogen peroxide (3%)
- Petroleum jelly
- Rectal thermometer
- Rubber gloves
- Rubbing alcohol
- Scissors
- Tourniquet
- Towel
- Tweezers

33

average temperature of the dog is approximately 101.5°F, but there may be normal variation of a degree or so either way, so taking your pet's temperature before he is sick is a good way of establishing what his "baseline" is.

MEDICATING YOUR BEAGLE

If your vet sends you home with medication for your pet for whatever reason, have him or her demonstrate how to administer it.

If you have to give your hound a pill, put him on a table to get him closer to your eye level and immobilize him somewhat. With one hand, grasp the upper part of the muzzle and open his mouth. If you intentionally put his lips between his teeth and your fingers, he will be more reluctant to close his mouth before you are ready. With your other hand, place the pill as far back on his tongue as possible, taking care not to let it fall off to the side, where it may be bitten or expelled rather than swallowed. Close his mouth and hold his muzzle upright while stroking his throat to encourage swallowing. Keep doing this until you are sure he has swallowed. If your pet spits the pill out, keep at it until you succeed.

Liquid medications are pretty rare these days, and if you can't add it to the feed, ask your vet for a syringe (minus the needle). This is a much more controlled method of administering liquids than spoons, but the principle is the same. Here you want to keep his mouth closed, only opening the lips at the corner of his mouth. You then inject or pour the liquid in as you tilt the head back slightly. And you keep the muzzle closed until he swallows.

CHAPTER FOUR

Positively Nutritious

The nutritional needs of a dog will change throughout her lifetime. It is necessary to be aware of these changes not only for proper initial growth to occur, but also so your dog can lead a healthy life for many years.

Before bringing your puppy home, ask the breeder for the puppy's feeding schedule and information about what and how much she is used to eating. Maintain this regimen for at least the first few days before gradually changing to a schedule that is more in line with the family's lifestyle. The breeder may supply you with a small quantity of the food the puppy has been eating. Use this or have your own supply of the same food ready when you bring home your puppy.

After the puppy has been with you for three days and has become acclimated to her new environment, you can begin a gradual food change. Add a portion of the new food to the usual food. Add a little more of the new food each day until it has entirely replaced the previous diet. This gradual change will prevent an upset stomach and diarrhea. The total amount of food to be fed at each meal will remain the same at this stage of the puppy's life.

LIFE-STAGE FEEDING

Puppies and adolescent dogs require a much higher intake of protein, calories and nutrients than adult dogs due to the demands of their rapidly developing bodies. Most commercial brands of dry kibble meet these requirements and are well balanced for proper growth. The majority of puppy foods now available are so carefully planned that it is unwise to attempt to add anything other than water to them.

The major ingredients of most dry dog foods are chicken, beef or lamb by-products and corn, wheat or rice. The higher the meat content, the higher the protein percentage, palatability and digestibility of the food. Protein percentages in puppy food are usually between 25 and 30 percent. There are many advantages of dry foods over semimoist and canned dog foods for puppies and normal, healthy adult Beagles.

It is best to feed meals that are primarily dry food because the chewing action involved in eating a dry food is better for the health of the teeth and gums. Dry food is also less expensive than canned food of equal quality.

Dogs whose diets are based on canned or soft foods have a greater likelihood of developing calcium deposits and gum disease. Canned or semimoist foods do serve certain functions, however. As a supplement to dry dog food, in small portions, canned or semimoist foods can be useful to stimulate appetites and aid in weight gain. But unless very special conditions exist they are not the best way for a dog to meet her food needs.

Puppies and adolescent dogs require a high intake of protein, calories and nutrients to fuel their rapidly developing bodies.

WHAT'S BEST FOR YOUR BEAGLE

What complicates feeding our house Beagles so much is that we humans equate food with love, and our little hounds are too smart to tell us anything different. Consequently, we find ourselves letting our little pals lick our plates, eat the few odds and ends in the fridge we are suspicious or tired of, clean up the spills on the kitchen floor and so on, until our once svelte little hound starts looking like an overstuffed sausage! If we really love them, we will select a good quality, nutrient-dense dry dog food and feed nothing but that every day for the rest of their lives with goodies added only in moderation.

The Beagle has a wonderful appetite, and it is a rare Beagle who is a picky eater, compared to other small dogs. When people worry that their pet's diet is too boring, they are projecting their own feelings into a situation that is perfectly fine with the Beagle. Our concern should be finding a food that is convenient to feed, is completely balanced so that no supplements are necessary, is nutrient-dense so that less food is consumed and therefore less stool volume is generated

Feeding your Beagle dry food helps keep her teeth and gums healthy.

TO SUPPLEMENT OR NOT TO SUPPLEMENT?

If you're feeding your dog a diet that's correct for her developmental stage and she's alert, healthy-looking and neither over- nor underweight, you don't need to add supplements. These include table scraps as well as vitamins and minerals. In fact, a growing puppy is in danger of developing musculoskeletal disorders by oversupplementation. If you have any concerns about the nutritional quality of the food you're feeding, discuss them with your veterinarian.

GROWTH STAGE FOODS

Once upon a time, there was puppy food and there was adult dog food. Now there are foods for puppies, young adults/active dogs, less active dogs and senior citizens. What's the difference between these foods? They vary by the amounts of nutrients they provide for the dog's growth stage/activity level.

Less active dogs don't need as much protein or fat as growing, active dogs; senior dogs don't need some of the nutrients vital to puppies. By feeding a high-quality food that's appropriate for your dog's age and activity level, you're benefiting your dog and yourself. Feed too much protein to a couch potato and she'll have energy to spare, which means a few more trips around the block will be needed to burn it off. Feed an adult diet to a puppy, and risk growth and development abnormalities that could affect her for a lifetime.

and is reasonably priced so that we don't have to restructure our family grocery budget.

DIFFERENT DOGS NEED DIFFERENT DIETS

There has been considerable research over the past few years to suggest that nutrient requirements change according to age, condition, activity level, gestation, lactation and so on, and this only makes sense on an intuitive level. A hound who runs hundreds of miles a week hunting is going to burn more calories than a Beagle couch potato. Also, if that same hunting Beagle is kept in an unheated kennel, a certain number of calories will be used just to maintain body temperature.

38

Feeding your Beagle table scraps encourages bad manners and may result in weight problems.

While the protein requirements may not change that much, the energy difference must come either from additional carbohydrates or from fat. Fat has more calories on a dry-weight basis than either protein or carbohydrates, so it is the logical choice for supplementing the diets of hardworking animals.

Advances in feed manufacturing techniques have made it possible to incorporate higher levels of fat into extruded dog foods than in the past, thereby eliminating the need for the dog owner to add it on after the fact, which used to throw the correct nutritional proportions out of balance.

How Much to Feed?

If you take the recommendation of the breeder in selecting the food, keep in mind that the amounts they feed are based on the activity levels of their dogs in their geographical area. Similarly, the recommended feeding quantities as they appear on the bag are guidelines. Some Beagles will get fat on one cup of premium food a day, and another might require twice that just to keep her ribs from showing. This means you will

Food Allergies

If your puppy or dog seems to itch all the time for no apparent reason, she could be allergic to one or more ingredients in her food. This is not uncommon, and it's why many foods contain lamb and rice instead of beef, wheat or soy. Have your dog tested by your veterinarian, and be patient while you strive to identify and eliminate the allergens from your dog's food (or environment).

have to use your own judgment after getting input from the vet, breeder and feed store.

A well-fed Beagle will always be a *bit* hungry, so that is not a clue as to the proper amount to feed. The rule of thumb as to whether your Beagle is the correct weight is that you should be able to feel her ribs

You should be able to feel (but not see) the ribs of a well-fed, fit Beagle.

but not see them. If she is free of parasites and kept reasonably clean, there should be a "bloom" on her coat that comes with just the right amount of subcutaneous fat.

Should you feed the meal wet or dry? There are pluses and minuses to each method, and you will have to determine what works best for you and your Beagle. Feeding wet usually means either moistening or soaking the dry food in warm water or broth for a few minutes. This method is recommended for young puppies, whose dentition may not be up to crunching down their meals easily. Advocates of wet feeding believe it results in less bloating. It may also increase palatability and digestibility—considerations more important for puppies than for adults.

Dry feeding requires no time delay and may help slow down a hound who would otherwise gulp down her food. It may also be better for your pet's dental health. Also, on those rare occasions when your pet doesn't immediately clean her plate, you needn't be concerned with spoilage.

HOW MANY MEALS A DAY?

Individual dogs vary in how much they should eat to maintain a desired body weight—not too fat, but not too thin. Puppies need several meals a day, while older dogs may need only one. Determine how much food keeps your adult dog looking and feeling her best. Then decide how many meals you want to feed with that amount. Like us, most dogs love to eat, and offering two meals a day is more enjoyable for them. If you're worried about overfeeding, make sure you measure correctly and abstain from adding tidbits to the meals.

Whether you feed one or two meals, only leave your dog's food out for the amount of time it takes her to eat it—ten minutes, for example. Free-feeding (when food is available any time) and leisurely meals encourage picky eating. Don't worry if your dog doesn't finish all her dinner in the allotted time. She'll learn she should.

KEEP YOUR BEAGLE SLIM

Finally, remember that obesity will shorten your Beagle's lifespan, increase the likelihood of health problems, and in general reduce her quality of life. The occasional biscuit, bit of meat or cooked egg can be given as a special treat, but on the whole "tough love" will result in a happier, healthier Beagle.

CHAPTER FIVE

Putting on the Dog

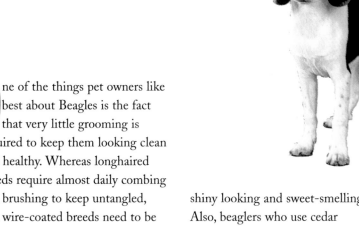

One of the things pet owners like best about Beagles is the fact that very little grooming is required to keep them looking clean and healthy. Whereas longhaired breeds require almost daily combing and brushing to keep untangled, and wire-coated breeds need to be clipped or plucked three or four times a year, our little hounds are the quintessential low-maintenance canines.

Many hunting Beagles go an entire lifetime without seeing the inside of a grooming salon—or even the basement sink! Assuming they are properly fed and kept in a clean environment, the occasional "herbal bath" obtained by running them through wet vegetation keeps them shiny looking and sweet-smelling. Also, beaglers who use cedar shavings in the hound's sleeping quarters never have to worry about their Beagle offending anyone with "doggy" odor.

KEEPING CLEAN IS BEING CLEAN

The first essential in having a well-groomed Beagle is keeping his environment clean. When well-intentioned but misinformed people

Beagles are low-maintenance dogs; a little grooming keeps them looking clean and healthy.

BATHE ONLY FOR BEAUTY

It is not only unnecessary to bathe your Beagle, it is counterproductive, since it will rob the hound's skin of the oils and exacerbate the tendency of some house Beagles to have dry skin and the itchiness that goes with it. This is especially true in the winter, when the dry heated air in the house is a problem for humans as well.

Bathing should be reserved for emergencies only, such as when your friend has been sprayed by a skunk or has rolled in something malodorous. In the case of the skunk attack, the thorough soaking with tomato juice need not include soap or detergent and therefore more closely approximates "marinating" than bathing.

When you do bathe your Beagle, use tepid water rather than hot, as dogs don't tolerate very warm water as well as we do. Use a commercial dog shampoo, and follow the directions on the bottle. Use a shampoo that is effective against fleas and ticks, and most will have some kind of conditioner to put back some of the moisture inevitably removed by bathing.

tell you that Beagles are "smelly," it is usually because they have encountered members of the breed who were kept in less than optimal conditions.

Beagles who for whatever reason must spend any time out-of-doors should have a small weatherproof house with a removable roof to make it easy to clean, disinfect and change the bedding. Cedar shavings are purported to help reduce the flea population on your pet (in addition to being a pleasant canine cologne).

Be sure to rinse thoroughly and keep your pet indoors (except during the warm months) until thoroughly dry. Even if the weather is warm enough to let your Beagle "sun-dry," it is often better to confine him until completely dry, as he is likely to go out of his way to get dirty by rolling and rubbing up against everything in sight for the first hour or so after a bath.

Be careful in bathing to avoid getting the suds or water in your pet's eyes or ears. Some people put cotton or mineral oil in the hound's ears and mineral oil or eye ointment in the eyes before bathing, but I prefer to just be careful.

When you are not bathing your Beagle—which should be most of the time—regular grooming will consist of frequent brushing. This routine is best established while your puppy is small and if introduced properly should be pleasurable for both you and your pet.

BRUSHING WORKS WONDERS

Unlike the longhaired breeds whose coats are prone to tangling and matting, the Beagle's coat must be brushed more to bring out the shine,

Even though your Beagle may spend lots of time outdoors, baths are only necessary if he's encountered a skunk or rolled in something stinky.

43

and gently stimulate the skin. For this purpose, a wire carding brush is often used. With short wire bristles set in soft rubber, this brush is gentle on the skin and is useful in thinning the undercoat during those times when your hound is shedding.

Shedding blades, which resemble a looped saw blade with a handle, are also handy in removing dead hair during shedding. Some people have a personal preference for natural bristle brushes, and while these may not be as efficient as the other two tools described, efficiency is not

A well-brushed coat makes your Beagle look and feel good, and will reduce shedding on those occasions when he is allowed on the furniture!

the only consideration in grooming. It is also a time to bond with your pet, and therefore should feel good as well as make him look good.

THE GREAT HOUND GLOVE

A fourth tool for regular grooming is the hound glove, a squarish-shaped mitten with short bristles on one side. Petting or massaging your Beagle with the hound glove on your hand meets his needs for human interaction and stroking, cleans his coat, and stimulates his skin at the same time.

Towels are commonly used in the grooming of hounds and, in addition to their obvious utility in tidying up the dog after a walk in the rain or snow, are often used as the final polishing tool after the brush and glove. The towel can also be lightly moistened with various pleasant-smelling insect repellents when called for and used to rub these medications into the coat in a way that is less upsetting to the hound than spray application would be.

A flea comb, a fine-toothed metal comb, is useful when fleas are a problem. Since fleas are pretty active and mobile, it is not likely that this tool will be of much help until the fleas have been killed or immobilized with a spray or dip.

No clipping is required with Beagles, but show Beagles are trimmed with scissors and thinning shears when excess hair detracts from the clean lines so desirable in a show dog. The whiskers are usually trimmed for show, but a field trial beagler wouldn't think of tampering with any of his hound's sensory devices.

NAILS NEED TRIMMING

If you begin trimming your Beagle's nails when your puppy is small, it should never become the ordeal it

44

seems to be for some people—sometimes requiring the vet to cut them!

Begin trimming nails when your puppy can be held easily under one arm and therefore be less mobile than if on a table. On a young puppy, a human-type fingernail clipper will work; then later you can switch to the kinds sold in pet shops. These are relatively inexpensive, so it often pays to buy the top-quality model. If you begin when your hound is young, you will better be able to see the "quick," or the blood supply to the nail, as the nails are more transparent in puppies.

Don't panic if you accidentally cut the nail too short. Just apply a little pressure or styptic powder, and keep the pup immobilized until the bleeding stops.

KEEP THOSE EARS CLEAN

The Beagle's ears require regular monitoring, and regular cleaning will help prevent things like ear mites, canker or ear infections. Breeds with pendulous ears are more prone to ear problems, so here a bit of routine maintenance is in order. About once a month, put a drop or two of plain mineral oil in each ear and, with your thumb and forefinger, gently massage

QUICK AND PAINLESS NAIL CLIPPING

This is possible if you make a habit out of handling your dog's feet and giving your dog treats when you do. When it's time to clip nails, go through the same routine, but take your clippers and snip off just the ends of the nail—clip too far down and you'll cut into the "quick," the nerve center, hurting your dog and causing the nail to bleed. Clip two nails at a time while you're getting your dog used to the procedure, and you'll soon be doing all four feet quickly and easily.

45

Regular exercise will help keep your Beagle's nails trim, but you should expect to clip them regularly anyway.

GROOMING TOOLS

pin brush	scissors
slicker brush	nail clippers
flea comb	tooth-cleaning equipment
towel	shampoo
mat rake	conditioner
grooming glove	clippers

the ear at its base, nearest the skull, until you hear a squishing sound. Then, using a cotton ball, gently swab out the ear, taking care not to delve too deeply into the ear canal. This procedure should take only a few minutes if done regularly, and if it helps you avoid ear problems, it is well worth it.

TOOTH CARE

More and more research is being done that suggests that canine dental care is more than just an aesthetic issue. Calculus left unchecked will eventually cause gum disease and tooth loss. There is also some evidence that it will shorten your pet's life by contributing to kidney disease. Your vet can advise on the best ways to prevent this buildup and can also clean your hound's teeth for you, but as this can be a fairly expensive procedure, you will want to learn all you can do to prevent problems before they become serious.

Biscuits, chew toys or treats aid in cleaning your Beagle's teeth. Many vets also are advising pet owners to brush their pet's teeth and use the canine equivalent of floss. If you subscribe to this practice, begin doing it when your puppy is young and impressionable; otherwise it will be an ordeal.

In summary, the Beagle is one of the easiest breeds to keep well-groomed, and this grooming has numerous payoffs in areas other than the good looks of your pet.

Instituted early and made a regular part of your interaction with your Beagle, grooming will extend the life and improve the quality of life of your best canine friend.

CHAPTER SIX

Measuring Up

WHAT IS A BREED STANDARD?

A breed standard—a detailed description of an individual breed—is meant to portray the *ideal* specimen of that breed. This includes ideal structure, temperament, gait and type—all aspects of the dog. Because the standard describes an ideal specimen, it isn't based on any particular dog. It is a concept against which judges compare actual dogs and breeders strive to produce dogs. At a dog show, the dog that wins is the one that comes closest, in the judge's opinion, to the standard for her breed.

The Beagle standard was developed and approved by the National

Beagle Club of America, whose mission since its inception in 1887 has been "to improve the Beagle in the field and on the bench." Therefore, the standard describes not only a beautiful hound, but one who has been designed to do her job both effectively and tirelessly.

This chapter will attempt to explicate the appearance and personality of the breed, according to the AKC standard. It is important

The breed standard describes the ideal Beagle: a handsome hound who has been designed to do her job both effectively and tirelessly.

48

to keep in mind when reading the standard and trying to match one's own Beagle to it that the standard describes an *ideal* Beagle, and some sections are geared toward a show interpretation.

What follow are descriptions of the ideal Beagle. Excerpts from the breed standard appear in italics, and are followed by an explanation of their statements.

THE OFFICIAL STANDARD FOR THE BEAGLE

The following is the standard approved by the American Kennel Club in 1957.

Head

*The skull should be fairly long, slightly domed at the occiput, with cranium broad and full. **Ears**—Ears set on moderately low, long, reaching when drawn out nearly, if not quite, to the end of the nose; fine in texture, fairly broad—with almost entire absence of erectile power—setting close to the head, with the forward edge slightly inturning to the cheek—rounded at the tip. **Eyes**—Eyes large, set well apart— soft and houndlike—expression gentle and pleading; of a brown or hazel color. **Muzzle**—Muzzle of medium length—straight and square-cut—the stop moderately defined. **Jaws**—Jaws level. Lips free from flews; nostrils large and open. **Defects**—A very flat skull, narrow across the top; excess of dome, eyes small, sharp or terrier-like, or prominent and protruding; muzzle long, snipy or cut away decidedly below the eyes, or very short. Roman-nosed, or upturned giving a dish-faced expression. Ears short, set on high or with a tendency to rise above the point of origin.*

When the cranium is described as "full and broad," we are of course assuming it is to be full of brains, and the wide nostrils and moderately long muzzle should help with the

Your Beagle should have wide nostrils and a long muzzle to help her follow the scent of her quarry.

olfactory wizardry required of a hound expected to follow the trail of the rabbit, the game animal that leaves the least amount of scent of any quarry.

What about the concern about the eyes? We may speculate that part of the reason derives from the Foxhound, of which our Beagle is a "miniature." Masters of Foxhounds were also horsemen, and the "kind eye" is one measure of a trustworthy mount. Regardless of the origin of this element of the standard, the "typical" Beagle expression is one of the things that makes the Beagle so compelling. If eyes are, indeed, the windows to the soul, then looking into a Beagle's eyes should reveal the

honesty, loyalty, affection and intelligence that make the Beagle so beloved in the field, in the home and in the show ring. These eyes are also responsible for Beagles being given too many treats, but we will discuss that later.

Body

NECK AND THROAT

Neck rising free and light from the shoulders, strong in substance yet not loaded, of medium length. The throat clean and free from folds of skin; a slight wrinkle below the angle of the jaw, however, may be allowable. Defects— A thick, short cloddy neck carried on a line with the top of the shoulders.

The Beagle's eyes reveal her loyal and intelligent nature.

Throat showing dewlap and folds of skin to a degree termed "throatiness."

SHOULDERS AND CHEST

*Shoulders sloping—clean, muscular, not heavy or loaded—conveying the idea of freedom of action with activity and strength. Chest deep and broad, but not broad enough to interfere with the free play of the shoulders. **Defects**— Straight, upright shoulders. Chest disproportionately wide or with lack of depth.*

BACK, LOIN AND RIBS

*Back short, muscular and strong. Loin broad and slightly arched, and the ribs well sprung, giving abundance of lung room. **Defects**—Very long or swayed or roached back. Flat, narrow loin, flat ribs.*

FORELEGS AND FEET

***Forelegs**—Straight with plenty of bone in proportion to the size of he hound. Pasterns short and straight. **Feet**—Close, round and firm. Pad full and hard. **Defects**—Out at elbows. Knees knuckled over forward, or bent backward. Forelegs crooked or Dachshund-like. Feet long, open or spreading.*

HIPS, THIGHS, HIND LEGS AND FEET

*Hips and thighs strong and well muscled, giving abundance of propelling power. Stifles strong and well let down. Hocks firm, symmetrical and moderately bent. Feet close and firm. **Defects**—Cowhocks, or straight hocks. Lack of muscle and propelling power. Open feet.*

It is understandable why the authors of the standard would put such emphasis on the body and running gear of Beagles. Originally they were expected to hunt for hours over all types of terrain, to overtake through courage, patience and persistence a hare capable of reaching speeds of forty miles per hour.

Not able to attain speeds like that themselves, the little hounds had to use their highly developed sense of smell, pack instincts and intelligence to stay in the chase till their quarry tired. Therefore, all the emphasis is on strength, propelling power, sound, firm feet, freedom of action, ample lung capacity and other elements decidedly structural rather than cosmetic.

TAIL

Set moderately high; carried gaily, but not turned forward over the back; with slight curve; short as compared with size of the hound; with brush. **Defects**—*A long tail. Teapot curve or inclined forward from the root. Rat tail with absence of brush.*

COAT

A close, hard, hound coat of medium length. **Defects**—*A short, thin coat, or of a soft quality.*

COLOR

Any true hound color.

If we examine the standard in more detail, we may find it interesting to note that color and markings are not considered important. There is a saying, "A good horse cannot be a bad color," and this applies to Beagles as well. Beagles come in

The Beagle's strength and endurance enable her to hunt for many hours over all types of terrain.

many colors, including the most common black, tan and white; lemon and white; red and white; chocolate (or liver), tan and white; and some colors whose names come from out of the hunting past, like "Belvoir Tan" and "Badger Pie."

Many of the Beagles appearing in photos taken in this country early in this century were predominately white, with the occasional patch of color, but the majority of today's Beagles are black, tan and white, with a tendency to have solid black backs, which is described as being

THE AMERICAN KENNEL CLUB

Familiarly referred to as "the AKC," the American Kennel Club is a nonprofit organization devoted to the advancement of purebred dogs. The AKC maintains a registry of recognized breeds and adopts and enforces rules for dog events including shows, obedience trials, field trials, hunting tests, lure coursing, herding, earthdog trials, agility and the Canine Good Citizen program. It is a club of clubs, established in 1884 and composed, today, of over 500 autonomous dog clubs throughout the United States. Each club is represented by a delegate; the delegates make up the legislative body of the AKC, voting on rules and electing directors. The American Kennel Club maintains the Stud Book, the record of every dog ever registered with the AKC, and publishes a variety of materials on purebred dogs, including a monthly magazine, books and numerous educational pamphlets. For more information, contact the AKC at the address listed in Chapter 9, "Resources."

GENERAL APPEARANCE

A miniature Foxhound, solid and big for his inches, with the wear-and-tear look of the hound that can last in the chase and follow his quarry to the death.

Varieties

There shall be two varieties:
 ***Thirteen Inch**—which shall be for hounds not exceeding 13 inches in height.*
 ***Fifteen Inch**—which shall be for hounds over 13 but not exceeding 15 inches in height.*

Disqualification

Any hound measuring more than 15 inches shall be disqualified.

The key to evaluating a Beagle's conformation is in assessing the overall picture. Basically, a good Beagle will be "square" in appearance; have good bone; a straight front; a deep chest with a pronounced "tuck-up"; strong well-angulated hindquarters and a good head with a pleasing expression. There should be symmetry and fluidity in her motion. Proportion and balance are important dimensions in assessing good Beagle type (it is

"black blanketed." If a hound has flecks of color either tan (red) or muted black (blue), this coloring is called *ticking*, and when one refers to a "Blueticked" Beagle, the name refers only to the coloration and not to the Coonhound of the same name.

possible to have a hound with acceptable parts that just are not knit together properly). Very often, a relative novice to the breed can select the best hound in a show ring or the best puppy in a litter just by assessing proportion and balance.

There is no perfect Beagle in the world; every dog has some fault or weakness. It is the *overall* appearance and attitude that are most important in evaluating the Beagle. There are many faults and a few disqualifications in the Beagle standard, and while they might affect a dog if she were to be entered in a dog show, they will have no bearing on a dog's ability to be a good companion. Remember this when reading the standard and applying it to your own dog.

CHAPTER SEVEN

A Matter of Fact

UNRAVELING THE BEAGLE'S PAST

Some people would like to claim that the Beagle was Adam's hunting dog (but not his food taster), and others would prefer that the Beagle "just growed," leaving the historical antecedents of the modern Beagle to fend for themselves.

Somewhere in between these two camps, we should be able to re-create a satisfactory history of today's Beagle. Those who would prefer a more exhaustive history can repair to the library and find volumes to sift through.

The Beagle is a scenthound bred over the centuries to hunt hare. We say *hare* rather than *rabbit* because in Europe and England, where much of this history took place, it is the European hare that is the quarry.

THE HUNTING HOUND

In ancient times small dogs were used to hunt the hare, but, as the object was meat on the table rather than sport, not much consideration was placed on type or style of hunting. Basically the dogs helped locate the hare, a creature of open fields, and drove it into long nets for capture. There are written records of such hunts in ancient Greece, predating the birth of Christ.

Even in the beginning, two distinct classes of canine were used to hunt the hare (or other quarry): scenthounds, like the Beagle and sight (or "gaze") hounds, like the modern Greyhound and Whippet. The former were members of sizable packs, and the latter hunted either singly or in very small groups.

The Beagle is an ancient breed that was used to hunt hare.

FROM DEER TO HARE

In England, the deer belonged to the king (remember Robin Hood?), and the most noble form of venery (hunting) was stag hunting. Large hounds similar to modern Foxhounds were the hound of choice. If you weren't king but were "landed" well enough to maintain hounds, horses and the staff to care for both, you had the option of hunting the ever-abundant and (much demonized) fox, which was considered vermin and therefore not worthy of royal

attention. At the bottom of this ladder were the lesser noblemen who were still keen to hunt but may have lacked the resources or country to support a pack of Foxhounds. These became the first modern beaglers.

When we say the Beagle is a miniature Foxhound, implicit in that statement is that the history of the Beagle is inextricably intertwined with that of the evolution of the Foxhound, and the two matured about the same time—roughly 200 years ago.

Issues about standardizing the size, type and hunting style were

Beagle lovers have always wanted beautiful, functional hounds.

THE BEAGLE IN AMERICA

In America, the Beagle kept a rather low profile until the mid–nineteenth century. Actually, a popular favorite of the colonists was the Black-and-Tan Hound, a close relative of the modern Kerry Beagle of Ireland, more Foxhound or Harrier-sized, but a multipurpose hound capable of hunting small and large game, day or night.

The rabbit hound of that time was probably not much to look at, resembling a Dachshund more than a modern Beagle. But, then, consider the needs of the early settlers: A hound who helped put meat on the table was of primary importance.

Meanwhile, the Foxhound is doing just fine, thank you, with advocates no less influential than George Washington, who continued foxhunting through much of the Revolutionary War!

Also, several distinct American strains of Foxhounds were being developed to match the different conditions seen on this continent.

The improvement of the American Beagle began in earnest with the importation in the mid–to late nineteenth century of foundation

thrashed about for years, and it is interesting to note that many of the same issues are hotly debated in the world of Beagles today: How fast should a hound be? What is the best size? Which is more important, nose or looks?

With a number of packs hunting in different parts of the country, with different terrain and agricultural practices, Beagle diversity is likely to have reached its peak before the advent of motor cars or even semiconvenient railway travel, when it became easier for packs to get together and compare notes.

stock from the best working packs in England.

General Richard Rowett of Illinois was the first to begin this trend, and it was beaglers like General Rowett, who were interested in a beautiful, functional hound, who formed the core group of breeders who were to develop the present standard (which is actually little different from the English standard) and form the club known today as the National Beagle Club (NBC) of America.

As with any breed, there were those breeders who were able to maintain large numbers of animals and thereby have a greater opportunity to have an impact on the breed. So it is not surprising that in the records of the early winners both in the field and in the shows, the packs registered with the NBC did extremely well.

COMPETING WITH BEAGLES

The first Beagle field trial was held in Hyannis, Massachusetts, in 1888, one year after the formation of the NBC, and Beagle field trials have been going strong ever since. Beagle specialty shows began soon after, in

Beagles require stamina, a sound constitution and good temperament to keep hunting all day if they have to.

WHERE DID DOGS COME FROM?

It can be argued that dogs were right there at man's side from the beginning of time. As soon as human beings began to document their existence, the dog was among their drawings and inscriptions. Dogs were not just friends, they served a purpose: There were dogs to hunt birds, pull sleds, herd sheep, burrow after rats—even sit in laps! What your dog was originally bred to do influences the way he behaves. The American Kennel Club recognizes over 140 breeds, and there are hundreds more distinct breeds around the world. To make sense of the breeds, they are grouped according to their size or function. The AKC has seven groups:

1) Sporting, 2) Working, 3) Herding,

4) Hounds, 5) Terriers, 6) Toys,

7) Nonsporting

Can you name a breed from each group? Here's some help: (1) Golden Retriever; (2) Doberman Pinscher; (3) Collie; (4) Beagle; (5) Scottish Terrier; (6) Maltese; and (7) Dalmatian. All modern domestic dogs (*Canis familiaris*) are related, however different they look, and are all descended from *Canis lupus*, the grey wolf.

1891, and while there may have been less than a total meeting of the minds between the two groups, there were numerous individuals and packs that strove to "do it all."

Early into the twentieth century, beaglers in New England who hunted the Varying Hare (Snowshoe Hare) developed their own form of testing hound merit by casting the entire class of hounds entered and competing them in a large pack for up to twelve hours. Whereas the cottontail is a creature given to short bursts, who will run in a reasonably small territory for a short interval before seeking sanctuary in a stone wall or groundhog den, its big-footed cousin will stay aboveground and run almost indefinitely, often taking the hounds out of the hearing range of their handlers for an hour or more.

This type of competition rewarded stamina, sound constitution and also sound temperament, to a certain extent, since many hounds cannot tolerate the pressure of a large pack of hounds in full cry. Of course, the number of these trials was limited to the areas of the country where the Varying Hare was located.

A subjective review of the period would suggest that the real heyday of the Beagle in America was in the 1940s and '50s, when the sport of beagling and AKC registration of the

Beagle grew exponentially. There was still sufficient open country that it was practical for many sportsmen to keep a few Beagles for hunting the ever-plentiful cottontail and the reasonably abundant pheasant. Beagle clubs were popping up all over the country, with field trials at the club level that enticed rabbit hunters to enter their "brag dogs" and thereby enter the world of organized beagling.

The show Beagle had reached an amazing degree of refinement, even relative to hounds bred a decade before, and still there were breeders able to produce hounds capable of earning their championship in both AKC field trials and bench shows—thereby earning the ultimate title of Dual Champion (DC). In addition to that, numerous hounds were completing their Field Championship with wins both in brace trials on the tricky cottontail, and large pack trials on the elusive and long-running Varying Hare.

Also at this time, the NBC held its trials for its recognized packs during the same week it held its brace trial, often using the same judges for both events, and then a bench show for hounds who competed in the pack classes. The week of beagling would end with a three-hour Stake class, which tested a hound's endurance, nose and ability to cooperate as well as compete with other hounds.

SPLITTING FIELD AND SHOW BEAGLES

Aside from those few breeders dedicated to the dual-purpose hound, the gap grew ever wider between the field trial Beagle and the Beagle bred strictly with showing in mind. Sometime in the 1960s, a trend began in brace trials (the most popular form of competition at the time) to slow down the action.

The number of hounds competing in many of the most popular trials was so large that insufficient time was allocated to judge them as they would be judged under normal hunting conditions (that is, an entire day afield), so a more conservative hound who moved more slowly and thereby made fewer errors (remember the Southern Hound?) was favored over the faster, flashier hound who needed more time to settle down.

While there had been a number of famous field trial bloodlines then, such as Blue Cap, Yellow Creek, Shady Shore and Fish Creek, to name only a few, there were still hounds who earned their titles by *driving* a rabbit and outfooting their competition.

AND THEN CAME BOOGIE

All that changed with the appearance of a hound named FC (Field Champion) Wilcliffe Boogie. Boogie captured the beagling public's imagination like few other hounds ever have, and while there is no question that he was a *hunting* hound (he was used to hunt raccoon, fox and rabbits), he was a trailing type hound. So while other famous hounds, like FC Gray's

FAMOUS OWNERS OF THE BEAGLE

Charles Schulz

Roger Staubach

Eva Gabor

Barry Manilow

Mary Pickford

Linesman, were trailing hounds as opposed to driving hounds, people almost immediately began to line-breed and inbreed to Boogie, thereby fixing and even intensifying the driving trait.

Today the modern brace trial Beagle is a slow trailing specialist. In most cases, a single heat of a competition may last only a few minutes and cover less than 100 feet. The dog is judged for the absence of any mistakes rather than actual accomplishment in pursuing the rabbit.

The modern large-pack-on-hare hound has changed little over the years. He still must have the stamina and constitution to compete, although the time on game has been reduced. Few new clubs have been formed for this type of trial, again because of the geographical limitations of the natural range of the Snowshoe Hare.

In the early 1970s, a group of beaglers unhappy with the trend in American Kennel Club brace trials began meeting with representatives of the AKC to persuade them to acknowledge a different form of competition that would more closely simulate hunting conditions. Hounds would be run in small packs, required to search for their own game and tested for gun-shyness. This type of trial, known as small pack option (SPO), is the fastest growing phase of the sport of beagling today. One of the larger SPO groups—the United Beagle Gundog Federation—conducts trials where the grand final winner is determined by combining his scores from both the field and the bench portion of the trial, a real step forward in improving the total Beagle.

AMERICA'S FAVORITE PET

The pet Beagle in America has, in many ways, been a by-product of both field-bred and show-bred beagles. No serious breeder breeds a bitch just for the sake of selling the puppies, and he or she usually has a clear objective in mind. Show-bred puppies who the breeder guesses won't make the grade, or field-bred puppies who turn out too large or small to fit the breeder's program, end up in pet homes. Assuming the breeder is concerned with temperament, either type makes a suitable pet.

In the not-too-distant past, it was common for "Dad's hunting dog" to be the family pet, to live

Due to his small size and amazing sense of smell, the Beagle has been used to sniff out illegally imported goods.

61

in the house. This was also a time when more people lived on farms and Beagles lived a more liberated existence. Today, of course, a free-roaming Beagle would have a very short life expectancy, so many hunting Beagles live in outdoor kennels. The common myth among hunters that hunting Beagles are ruined by living in the house is not true. If reasonable care is taken in proper feeding, exercise and training, the Beagle better affiliated with his owner by virtue of more regular contact is more likely to perform better in the field than his counterpart in the backyard.

A KNOWLEDGEABLE NOSE

Aside from hunting, field trials and shows, Beagles have done well in recent years in Obedience Trials, and it seems that show and field lines perform equally well. Also, because of his small size, good disposition and outstanding sense of smell, the Beagle has been used by the United States Department of Agriculture (USDA) at international airports to sniff out illegally imported foodstuffs or plants, which could introduce animal or plant diseases into this country. Beagles who do this work are part of the USDA's Beagle Brigade. The cheerful little Beagle goes about his job without frightening the travelers and can fit into some tight spots a larger animal could not squeeze into.

The Beagle has proven to be extremely adaptable over the years, and that quality is undoubtedly one of the keys to his consistent popularity. This suggests that his future will be as interesting as his illustrious past.

CHAPTER EIGHT

On Good Behavior

by Ian Dunbar, Ph.D., MRCVS

T raining is the jewel in the crown—the most important aspect of doggy husbandry. There is no more important variable influencing dog behavior and temperament than the dog's education: A well-trained, well-behaved and good-natured puppydog is always a joy to live with, but an untrained and uncivilized dog can be a perpetual nightmare. Moreover, deny the dog an education and she will not have the opportunity to fulfill her own canine potential; neither will she have the ability to communicate effectively with her human companions.

Luckily, modern psychological training methods are easy, efficient, effective and, above all, considerably dog-friendly and user-friendly.

Doggy education is as simple as it is enjoyable. But before you can have a good time play-training with your new dog, you have to learn what to do and how to do it. There is no bigger variable influencing the success of dog training than the owner's experience and expertise. Before you embark on the dog's education, you must first educate yourself.

BASIC TRAINING FOR OWNERS

Ideally, basic owner training should begin well before you select your dog. Find out all you can about your chosen breed first, then master rudimentary training and handling skills. If you already have your puppydog, owner training is a dire emergency—the clock is ticking! Especially for puppies, the first few weeks at home are the most important and influential days in the dog's life. Indeed, the cause of most adolescent and adult problems may be traced back to the initial days the pup explores her new home. This is the time to establish the *status quo*—to teach the puppydog how you would like her to behave and so prevent otherwise quite predictable problems.

In addition to consulting breeders and breed books such as this one (which understandably have a positive breed bias), seek out as many pet owners with your breed as you can find. Good points are obvious. What you want to find out are the breed-specific problems, so you can nip them in the bud. In particular, you should talk to owners with adolescent dogs and make a list of all anticipated problems. Most important,

test drive at least half a dozen adolescent and adult dogs of your breed yourself. An 8-week-old puppy is deceptively easy to handle, but she will acquire adult size, speed and strength in just four months, so you should learn now what to prepare for.

Puppy and pet dog training classes offer a convenient venue to locate pet owners and observe dogs in action. For a list of suitable trainers in your area, contact the Association of Pet Dog Trainers (see chapter 9). You may also begin your basic owner training by observing other owners in class. Watch as many classes and test drive as many dogs as possible. Select an upbeat, dog-friendly, people-friendly, fun-and-games, puppydog pet training class to learn the ropes. Also, watch training videos and read training books. You must find out what to do and how to do it *before* you have to do it.

PRINCIPLES OF TRAINING

Most people think training comprises teaching the dog to do things such as sit, speak and roll over, but even a 4-week-old pup knows how to do these things already. Instead, the first step in training involves teaching the dog human words for each dog behavior and activity and for each aspect of the dog's environment. That way you, the owner, can more easily participate in the dog's domestic education by directing her to perform specific actions appropriately, that is, at the right time, in the right place and so on. Training opens communication channels, enabling an educated dog to at least understand her owner's requests.

In addition to teaching a dog what we want her to do, it is also necessary to teach her why she should do what we ask. Indeed, 95 percent of training revolves around motivating the dog to want to do what we want. Dogs often understand what their owners want; they just don't see the point of doing it—especially when the owner's repetitively boring and seemingly senseless instructions are totally at odds with much more pressing and exciting doggy distractions. It is not so much the dog that is being stubborn or dominant; rather, it is the owner who has failed to acknowledge the dog's needs and feelings and to approach training from the dog's point of view.

The Meaning of Instructions

The secret to successful training is learning how to use training lures to predict or prompt specific behaviors—to coax the dog to do what you want when you want. Any highly valued object (such as a treat or toy) may be used as a lure, which the dog will follow with her eyes and nose. Moving the lure in specific ways entices the dog to move her nose, head and entire body in specific ways. In fact, by learning the art of manipulating various lures, it is possible to teach the dog to assume virtually any body position and

OWNING A PARTY ANIMAL

It's a fact: The more of the world your puppy is exposed to, the more comfortable she'll be in it. Once your puppy's had her shots, start taking her everywhere with you. Encourage friendly interaction with strangers, expose her to different environments (towns, fields, beaches), and most important, enroll her in a puppy class where she'll get to play with other puppies. These simple, fun, shared activities will develop your pup into a confident extrovert, reliable around other people and other dogs.

perform any action. Once you have control over the expression of the dog's behaviors and can elicit any body position or behavior at will, you can easily teach the dog to perform on request.

Tell your dog what you want her to do, use a lure to entice her to respond correctly, then profusely praise and maybe reward her once she performs the desired action. For example, verbally request "Fido, sit!" while you move a squeaky toy upwards and backwards over the dog's muzzle (lure-movement and hand signal), smile knowingly as she looks up (to follow the lure) and sits down (as a result of canine anatomical engineering), then praise her to distraction ("Gooood Fido!"). Squeak the toy, offer a training treat and give your dog and yourself a pat on the back.

Being able to elicit desired responses over and over enables the owner to reward the dog over and over. Consequently, the dog begins to think training is fun. For example, the more the dog is rewarded for sitting, the more she enjoys sitting. Eventually the dog comes to realize that, whereas most sitting is appreciated, sitting immediately upon request usually prompts especially enthusiastic praise and a slew of high-level rewards. The dog begins to sit on cue much of the time, showing that she is starting to grasp the meaning of the owner's verbal request and hand signal.

Why Comply?

Most dogs enjoy initial lure-reward training and are only too happy to comply with their owners' wishes. Unfortunately, repetitive drilling without appreciative feedback tends to diminish the dog's enthusiasm until she eventually fails to see the point of complying anymore. Moreover, as the dog approaches adolescence she becomes more easily distracted as she develops other interests. Lengthy sessions with repetitive exercises tend to bore and demotivate both parties. If it's not fun, the owner doesn't do it and neither does the dog.

Integrate training into your dog's life: The greater number of training sessions each day and the shorter they are, the more willingly compliant your dog will become. Make sure to have a short (just a few seconds) training interlude before every enjoyable canine activity. For example, ask your dog to sit to greet people, to sit before you throw her Frisbee and to sit for her supper. Really, sitting is no different from a canine "Please." Also, include numerous short training interludes during every enjoyable canine pastime, for example, when playing with the dog or when she is running in the park. In this fashion, doggy distractions may be effectively converted into rewards for training. Just as all games have rules, fun becomes training . . . and training becomes fun.

Eventually, rewards actually become unnecessary to continue motivating your dog. If trained with consideration and kindness, performing the desired behaviors will become self-rewarding and, in a sense, your dog will motivate herself. Just as it is not necessary to reward a human companion during an enjoyable walk in the park, or following a game of tennis, it is hardly necessary to reward our best friend—the dog—for walking by our side or while playing fetch. Human company during enjoyable activities is reward enough for most dogs.

Even though your dog has become self-motivating, it's still good to praise and pet her a lot and offer rewards once in a while, especially for a job well done. And if for

no other reason, praising and rewarding others is good for the human heart.

Punishment

Without a doubt, lure-reward training is by far the best way to teach: Entice your dog to do what you want and then reward her for doing so. Unfortunately, a human shortcoming is to take the good for granted and to moan and groan at the bad. Specifically, the dog's many good behaviors are ignored while the owner focuses on punishing the dog for making mistakes. In extreme cases, instruction is limited to punishing mistakes made by a trainee dog, child, employee or husband, even though it has been proven punishment training is notoriously inefficient and ineffective and is decidedly unfriendly and combative. It teaches the dog that training is a drag, almost as quickly as it teaches the dog to dislike her trainer. Why treat our best friends like our worst enemies?

Punishment training is also much more laborious and time-consuming. Whereas it takes only a finite amount of time to teach a dog what to chew, for example, it takes much, much longer to punish the dog for each and every mistake. Remember, there is only one right way! So why not teach that right way from the outset?!

To make matters worse, punishment training causes severe lapses in the dog's reliability. Since it is obviously impossible to punish the dog each and every time she misbehaves, the dog quickly learns to distinguish between those times when she must comply (so as to avoid impending punishment) and those times when she need not comply because punishment is impossible. Such times include when the dog is off leash and 6 feet away, when the owner is otherwise engaged (talking to a friend, watching television, taking a shower, tending to the baby or chatting on the telephone) or when the dog is left at home alone.

Instances of misbehavior will be numerous when the owner is away because even when the dog complied in the owner's looming presence, she did so unwillingly. The dog was forced to act against her will, rather than molding her will to want to please. Hence, when the owner is absent, not only does the dog know she need not comply, she simply does not want to. Again,

the trainee is not a stubborn vindictive beast, but rather the trainer has failed to teach. Punishment training invariably creates unpredictable Jekyll and Hyde behavior.

TRAINER'S TOOLS

Many training books extol the virtues of a vast array of training paraphernalia and electronic and metallic gizmos, most of which are designed for canine restraint, correction and punishment, rather than for actual facilitation of doggy education. In reality, most effective training tools are not found in stores; they come from within ourselves. In addition to a willing dog, all you really need is a functional human brain, gentle hands, a loving heart and a good attitude.

In terms of equipment, all dogs do require a quality buckle collar to sport dog tags and to attach the leash (for safety and to comply with local leash laws). Hollow chew toys (like Kongs or sterilized longbones) and a dog bed or collapsible crate are musts for housetraining. Three additional tools are required:

1. specific lures (training treats and toys) to predict and prompt specific desired behaviors;

2. rewards (praise, affection, training treats and toys) to reinforce for the dog what a lot of fun it all is; and

3. knowledge—how to convert the dog's favorite activities and games (potential distractions to training) into "life-rewards," which may be employed to facilitate training.

The most powerful of these is knowledge. Education is the key! Watch training classes, participate in training classes, watch videos, read books, enjoy play-training with your dog and then your dog will say "Please," and your dog will say "Thank you!"

HOUSETRAINING

If dogs were left to their own devices, certainly they would chew, dig and bark for entertainment and then no doubt highlight a few areas of their living space with sprinkles of urine, in much the same way we decorate by hanging pictures. Consequently, when we ask a dog to live with us, we must teach her *where* she may dig, *where* she may perform her toilet duties, *what* she may chew and *when* she may

---

HOUSETRAINING 1-2-3

1. **Teach Where.** Take your puppy to the spot you want her to use every time you take her out to go. When she goes, praise her profusely!

2. **Control When.** Keep your puppy—and yourself—on a schedule so you're taking her out every hour and after meals. Take her to her spot, and when she uses it, praise!

3. **Prevent Mistakes.** When you can't supervise your puppy, confine her in a single room or in her crate (but don't leave her for too long!). Puppy-proof the area by laying down newspapers so that if she does make a mistake it won't matter. Take her out immediately upon your return, and praise when she uses her spot.

69

---

bark. After all, when left at home alone for many hours, we cannot expect the dog to amuse herself by completing crosswords or watching TV!

Also, it would be decidedly unfair to keep the house rules a secret from the dog, and then get angry and punish the poor critter for inevitably transgressing rules she did not even know existed. Remember: Without adequate education and guidance, the dog will be forced to establish her own rules—doggy rules—and most probably will be at odds with the owner's view of domestic living.

Since most problems develop during the first few days the dog is at home, prospective dog owners must be certain they are quite clear about the principles of house-training *before* they get a dog. Early misbehaviors quickly become established as the *status quo*—becoming firmly entrenched as hard-to-break bad habits, which set the precedent for years to come. Make sure to teach your dog good habits right from the start. Good habits are just as hard to break as bad ones!

Ideally, when a new dog comes home, try to arrange for someone to be present as much as possible during the first few days (for adult dogs) or weeks for puppies. With only a little forethought, it is surprisingly easy to find a puppy sitter, such as a retired person, who would be willing to eat from your refrigerator and watch your television while keeping an eye on the newcomer to encourage the dog to play with chew toys and to ensure she goes outside on a regular basis.

Potty Training

Follow these steps to teach the dog where she should relieve herself:

1. never let her make a single mistake;

2. let her know where you want her to go; and

3. handsomely reward her for doing so: "GOOOOOOOD DOG!!!" liver treat, liver treat, liver treat!

Preventing Mistakes

A single mistake is a training disaster, since it heralds many more in future weeks. And each time the dog soils the house, this further reinforces the dog's unfortunate preference for an indoor, carpeted toilet. Do not let an unhousetrained dog have full run of the house.

When you are away from home, or cannot pay full attention, confine the dog to an area where elimination is appropriate, such as an outdoor run or, better still, a small, comfortable indoor kennel with access to an outdoor run. When confined in this manner, most dogs will naturally housetrain themselves.

If that's not possible, confine the dog to an area, such as a utility room, kitchen, basement or garage, where elimination may not be desired in the long run but as an interim measure it is certainly preferable to doing it all around the house. Use newspaper to cover the floor of the dog's day room. The newspaper may be used to soak up the urine and to wrap up and dispose of the feces. Once your dog develops a preferred spot for eliminating, it is only necessary to cover that part of the floor with newspaper. The smaller papered area may then be moved (only a little each day) toward the door to the outside. Thus the dog will develop the tendency to go to the door when she needs to relieve herself.

Never confine an unhousetrained dog to a crate for long periods. Doing so would force the dog to soil the crate and ruin its usefulness as an aid for housetraining (see the following discussion).

Teaching Where

In order to teach your dog where you would like her to do her business, you have to be there to direct the proceedings—an obvious, yet often neglected, fact of life. In order to be there to teach the dog where

to go, you need to know *when* she needs to go. Indeed, the success of housetraining depends on the owner's ability to predict these times. Certainly, a regular feeding schedule will facilitate prediction somewhat, but there is nothing like "loading the deck" and influencing the timing of the outcome yourself!

Whenever you are at home, make sure the dog is under constant supervision and/or confined to a small area. If already well trained, simply instruct the dog to lie down in her bed or basket. Alternatively, confine the dog to a crate (doggy den) or tie-down (a short, 18-inch lead that can be clipped to an eye hook in the baseboard near her bed). Short-term close confinement strongly inhibits urination and defecation, since the dog does not want to soil her sleeping area. Thus, when you release the puppydog each hour, she will definitely need to urinate immediately and defecate every third or fourth hour. Keep the dog confined to her doggy den and take her to her intended toilet area each hour, every hour and on the hour. When taking your dog outside, instruct her to sit quietly before opening the door— she will soon learn to sit by the door when she needs to go out!

72

Teaching Why

Being able to predict when the dog needs to go enables the owner to be on the spot to praise and reward the dog. Each hour, hurry the dog to the intended toilet area in the yard, issue the appropriate instruction ("Go pee!" or "Go poop!"), then give the dog three to four minutes to produce. Praise and offer a couple of training treats when successful. The treats are important because many people fail to praise their dogs with feeling . . . and housetraining is hardly the time for understatement. So either loosen up and enthusiastically praise that dog: "Wuzzzer-wuzzer-wuzzer, hoooser good wuffer den? Hoooo went pee for Daddy?" Or say "Good dog!" as best you can and offer the treats for effect.

Following elimination is an ideal time for a spot of play-training in the yard or house. Also, an empty dog may be allowed greater freedom around the house for the next half hour or so, just as long as you keep an eye out to make sure she does not get into other kinds of mischief. If you are preoccupied and cannot pay full attention, confine the dog to her doggy den once more to enjoy a peaceful snooze or to play with her many chew toys.

If your dog does not eliminate within the allotted time outside—no biggie! Back to her doggy den, and then try again after another hour.

As I own large dogs, I always feel more relaxed walking an empty dog, knowing that I will not need to finish our stroll weighted down with bags of feces!

Beware of falling into the trap of walking the dog to get her to eliminate. The good ol' dog walk is such an enormous highlight in the dog's life that it represents the single biggest potential reward in domestic dogdom. However, when in a hurry, or during inclement weather, many owners abruptly terminate the walk the moment the dog has done her business. This, in effect, severely punishes the dog for doing the right thing, in the right place at the right time. Consequently, many dogs become strongly inhibited from eliminating outdoors because they know it will signal an abrupt end to an otherwise thoroughly enjoyable walk.

Instead, instruct the dog to relieve herself in the yard prior to going for a walk. If you follow the above instructions, most dogs soon learn to eliminate on cue. As soon as the dog eliminates, praise (and offer a treat or two)—"Good dog! Let's go walkies!" Use the walk as a re-ward for eliminating in the yard. If the dog does not go, put her back in her doggy den and think about a walk later on. You will find with a "No feces—no walk" policy, your dog will become one of the fastest defe-cators in the business.

If you do not have a backyard, instruct the dog to eliminate right outside your front door prior to the walk. Not only will this facilitate clean up and disposal of the feces in your own trash can but, also, the walk may again be used as a colossal reward.

CHEWING AND BARKING

Short-term close confinement also teaches the dog that occasional quiet moments are a reality of domestic living. Your puppydog is extremely impressionable during her first few weeks at home. Regular con-finement at this time soon exerts a calming influence over the dog's personality. Remember, once the dog is housetrained and calmer, there will be a whole lifetime ahead for the dog to enjoy full run of the house and garden. On the other hand, by letting the newcomer have unrestricted

access to the entire household and allowing her to run willy-nilly, she will most certainly develop a bunch of behavior problems in short order, no doubt necessitating confinement later in life. It would not be fair to remedially restrain and confine a dog you have trained, through neglect, to run free.

When confining the dog, make sure she always has an impressive array of suitable chew toys. Kongs and sterilized longbones (both readily available from pet stores) make the best chew toys, since they are hollow and may be stuffed with treats to heighten the dog's interest. For ex-ample, by stuffing the little hole at the top of a Kong with a small piece of freeze-dried liver, the dog will not want to leave it alone.

Remember, treats do not have to be junk food and they certainly should not represent extra calories. Rather, treats should be part of each dog's regular daily diet: Some food may be served in the dog's bowl for breakfast and dinner, some food may be used as training treats, and some food may be used for stuffing chew toys. I regularly stuff my dogs' many Kongs with different shaped biscuits and kibble. The kibble seems to fall out fairly easily, as do the oval-shaped

73

biscuits, thus rewarding the dog instantaneously for checking out the chew toys. The bone-shaped biscuits fall out after a while, rewarding the dog for worrying at the chew toy. But the triangular biscuits never come out. They remain inside the Kong as lures, maintaining the dog's fascination with her chew toy. To further focus the dog's interest, I always make sure to flavor the triangular biscuits by rubbing them with a little cheese or freeze-dried liver.

If stuffed chew toys are reserved especially for times the dog is confined, the puppydog will soon learn to enjoy quiet moments in her doggy den and she will quickly develop a chew-toy habit—a good habit! This is a simple autoshaping process; all the owner has to do is set up the situation and the dog all but trains herself—easy and effective. Even when the dog is given run of the house, her first inclination will be to indulge her rewarding chew-toy habit rather than destroy less-attractive household articles, such as curtains, carpets, chairs and compact disks. Similarly, a chew-toy chewer will be less inclined to scratch and chew herself excessively. Also, if the dog busies herself as a

recreational chewer, she will be less inclined to develop into a recreational barker or digger when left at home alone.

Stuff a number of chew toys whenever the dog is left confined and remove the extra-special-tasting treats when you return. Your dog will now amuse herself with her chew toys before falling asleep and then resume playing with her chew toys when she expects you to return. Since most owner-absent misbehavior happens right after you leave and right before your expected return, your puppydog will now be conveniently preoccupied with her chew toys at these times.

COME AND SIT

Most puppies will happily approach virtually anyone, whether called or not; that is, until they collide with adolescence and develop other more important doggy interests, such as sniffing a multiplicity of exquisite odors on the grass. Your mission, Mr./Ms. Owner, is to teach and reward the pup for coming reliably, willingly and happily when called— and you have just three months to get it done. Unless adequately reinforced, your puppy's tendency to

To teach come, call your dog, open your arms as a welcoming signal, wave a toy or a treat and praise for every step in your direction.

approach people will self-destruct by adolescence.

Call your dog ("Fido, come!"), open your arms (and maybe squat down) as a welcoming signal, waggle a treat or toy as a lure and reward the puppydog when she comes running. Do not wait to praise the dog until she reaches you—she may come 95 percent of the way and then run off after some distraction. Instead, praise the dog's first step towards you and continue praising enthusiastically for every step she takes in your direction.

When the rapidly approaching puppy dog is three lengths away from impact, instruct her to sit ("Fido, sit!") and hold the lure in front of you in an outstretched hand to prevent her from hitting you mid-chest and knocking you flat on your back! As Fido decelerates to nose the lure, move the treat upwards and backwards just over her muzzle with an upwards motion of your extended arm (palm upwards). As the dog looks up to follow the lure, she will sit down (if she jumps up, you are holding the lure too high). Praise the dog for sitting. Move backwards and call her again. Repeat this many times over, always praising when Fido comes and sits; on occasion, reward her.

For the first couple of trials, use a training treat both as a lure to entice the dog to come and sit and as a reward for doing so. Thereafter, try to use different items as lures and rewards. For example, lure the dog with a Kong or Frisbee but reward her with a food treat. Or lure the dog with a food treat but pat her and throw a tennis ball as a reward. After just a few repetitions, dispense with the lures and rewards; the dog will begin to respond willingly to your verbal requests and hand signals just for the prospect of praise from your heart and affection from your hands.

Instruct every family member, friend and visitor how to get the dog to come and sit. Invite people over for a series of pooch parties; do not keep the pup a secret—let other people enjoy this puppy, and let the pup enjoy other people. Puppy dog parties are not only fun, they easily attract a lot of people to help you train your dog. Unless you teach your dog how to meet people, that is, to sit for greetings, no doubt the dog will resort to jumping up. Then you and the visitors will get annoyed, and the dog will be punished. This is not fair. Send out those invitations for puppy parties and teach your dog to be mannerly and socially acceptable.

Even though your dog quickly masters obedient recalls in the house, her reliability may falter when playing in the backyard or local park. Ironically, it is the owner who has unintentionally trained the dog not to respond in these instances. By allowing the dog to play and run around and otherwise have a good time, but

then to call the dog to put her on leash to take her home, the dog quickly learns playing is fun but training is a drag. Thus, playing in the park becomes a severe distraction, which works against training. Bad news!

Instead, whether playing with the dog off leash or on leash, request her to come at frequent intervals— say, every minute or so. On most occasions, praise and pet the dog for a few seconds while she is sitting, then tell her to go play again. For especially fast recalls, offer a couple of training treats and take the time to praise and pet the dog enthusiastically before releasing her. The dog will learn that coming when called is not necessarily the end of the play session, and neither is it the end of the world; rather, it signals an enjoyable, quality time-out with the owner before resuming play once more. In fact, playing in the park now becomes a very effective life-reward, which works to facilitate training by reinforcing each obedient and timely recall. Good news!

SIT, DOWN, STAND AND ROLLOVER

Teaching the dog a variety of body positions is easy for owner and dog, impressive for spectators and extremely useful for all. Using lure-reward techniques, it is possible to train several positions at once to verbal commands or hand signals (which impress the socks off onlookers).

Sit and down—the two control commands—prevent or resolve nearly a hundred behavior problems. For example, if the dog happily and obediently sits or lies down when requested, she cannot jump on visitors, dash out the front door, run around and chase her tail, pester other dogs, harass cats or annoy family, friends or strangers. Additionally, "Sit" or "Down" are the best emergency commands for off-leash control.

It is easier to teach and maintain a reliable sit than maintain a reliable recall. Sit is the purest and simplest of commands—either the dog is sitting or she is not. If there is any change of circumstances or potential danger in the park, for example, simply instruct the dog to sit. If she sits, you have a number of options: Allow the dog to resume playing when she is safe, walk up and put the dog on leash or call the dog. The dog will be much more likely to come when called if she has

already acknowledged her compliance by sitting. If the dog does not sit in the park—train her to!

Stand and rollover-stay are the two positions for examining the dog. Your veterinarian will love you to distraction if you take a little time to teach the dog to stand still and roll over and play possum. Also, your vet bills will be smaller because it will take the veterinarian less time to examine your dog. The rollover-stay is an especially useful command and is really just a variation of the down-stay: Whereas the dog lies prone in the traditional down, she lies supine in the rollover-stay.

As with teaching come and sit, the training techniques to teach the dog to assume all other body positions on cue are user-friendly and dog-friendly. Simply give the appropriate request, lure the dog into the desired body position using a training treat or toy and then praise (and maybe reward) the dog as soon as she complies. Try not to touch the dog to get her to respond. If you teach the dog by guiding her into position, the dog will quickly learn that rump-pressure means sit, for example, but as yet you still have no control over your dog if she is just 6 feet away. It will still be necessary

Using a food lure to teach "Sit," "Down" and "Stand."
1) *"Phoenix, Sit."*
2) *Hand palm upwards, move lure up and back over dog's muzzle.*
3) *"Good sit, Phoenix!"*

4) *"Phoenix, Down."*
5) *Hand palm downwards, move lure down to lie between dog's forepaws.*
6) *"Phoenix, Off. Good down, Phoenix!"*

7) *"Phoenix, Sit!"*
8) *Palm upwards, move lure up and back, keeping it close to dog's muzzle.*
9) *"Good sit, Phoenix!"*

78

10) *"Phoenix, Stand!"*
11) *Move lure away from dog at nose height, then lower it a tad.*
12) *"Phoenix, Off! Good stand, Phoenix!"*

13) *"Phoenix, Down!"*
14) *Hand palm downwards, move lure down to lie between dog's forepaws.*
15) *"Phoenix, Off! Good down-stay, Phoenix!"*

16) *"Phoenix, Stand!"*
17) *Move lure away from dog's muzzle up to nose height.*
18) *"Phoenix, Off! Good stand-stay, Phoenix."*

to teach the dog to sit on request. So do not make training a time-consuming two-step process; instead, teach the dog to sit to a verbal request or hand signal from the outset. Once the dog sits willingly when requested, by all means use your hands to pet the dog when she does so.

To teach down when the dog is already sitting, say "Fido, down!," hold the lure in one hand (palm down) and lower that hand to the floor between the dog's forepaws. As the dog lowers her head to follow the lure, slowly move the lure away from the dog just a fraction (in front of her paws). The dog will lie down as she stretches her nose forward to follow the lure. Praise the dog when she does so. If the dog stands up, you pulled the lure away too far and too quickly.

When teaching the dog to lie down from the standing position, say "Down" and lower the lure to the floor as before. Once the dog has lowered her forequarters and assumed a play bow, gently and slowly move the lure towards the dog between her forelegs. Praise the dog as soon as her rear end plops down.

After just a couple of trials it will be possible to alternate sits and downs and have the dog energetically peform doggy push-ups. Praise the dog a lot, and after half a dozen or so push-ups reward the dog with a training treat or toy. You will notice the more energetically you move your arm—upwards (palm up) to get the dog to sit, and downwards (palm down) to get the dog to lie down—the more energetically the dog responds to your requests. Now try training the dog in silence and you will notice she has also learned to respond to hand signals. Yeah! Not too shabby for the first session.

To teach stand from the sitting position, say "Fido, stand," slowly move the lure half a dog-length away from the dog's nose, keeping it at nose level, and praise the dog as she stands to follow the lure. As soon as the dog stands, lower the lure to just beneath the dog's chin to entice her to look down; otherwise she will stand and then sit immediately. To prompt the dog to stand from the down position, move the lure half a dog-length upwards and away from the dog, holding the lure at standing nose height from the floor.

Teaching rollover is best started from the down position, with the dog lying on one side, or at least with both hind legs stretched out on the same side. Say "Fido, bang!"

and move the lure backwards and alongside the dog's muzzle to her elbow (on the side of her outstretched hind legs). Once the dog looks to the side and backwards, very slowly move the lure upwards to the dog's shoulder and backbone. Tickling the dog in the goolies (groin area) often invokes a reflex-raising of the hind leg as an appeasement gesture, which facilitates the tendency to roll over. If you move the lure too quickly and the dog jumps into the standing position, have patience and start again. As soon as the dog rolls onto her back, keep the lure stationary and mesmerize the dog with a relaxing tummy rub.

To teach rollover-stay when the dog is standing or moving, say "Fido, bang!" and give the appropriate hand signal (with index finger pointed and thumb cocked in true Sam Spade fashion), then in one fluid movement lure her to first lie down and then rollover-stay as above.

Teaching the dog to stay in each of the above four positions becomes a piece of cake after first teaching the dog not to worry at the toy or treat training lure. This is best accomplished by hand feeding dinner kibble. Hold a piece of kibble firmly in your hand and softly instruct "Off!"

Ignore any licking and slobbering for however long the dog worries at the treat, but say "Take it!" and offer the kibble the instant the dog breaks contact with her muzzle. Repeat this a few times, and then up the ante and insist the dog remove her muzzle for one whole second before offering the kibble. Then progressively refine your criteria and have the dog not touch your hand (or treat) for longer and longer periods on each trial, such as for two seconds, four seconds, then six, ten, fifteen, twenty, thirty seconds and so on.

The dog soon learns: (1) worrying at the treat never gets results, whereas (2) noncontact is often rewarded after a variable time lapse.

Teaching "Off!" has many useful applications in its own right. Additionally, instructing the dog not to touch a training lure often produces spontaneous and magical stays. Request the dog to stand-stay, for example, and not to touch the lure. At first set your sights on a short two-second stay before rewarding the dog. (Remember, every long journey begins with a single step.) However, on subsequent trials, gradually and progressively increase the length of stay required to receive a reward. In no time at all your dog will stand calmly for a minute or so.

RELEVANCY TRAINING

Once you have taught the dog what you expect her to do when requested to come, sit, lie down, stand, roll over and stay, the time is right to teach the dog why she should comply with your wishes. The secret is to have many (many) extremely short training interludes (two to five seconds each) at numerous (numerous) times during the course of the dog's day. Especially work with

TOYS THAT EARN THEIR KEEP

To entertain even the most distracted of dogs, while you're home or away, have a selection of the following toys on hand: hollow chew toys (like Kongs), sterilized hollow longbones and cubes or balls that can be stuffed with kibble. Smear peanut butter or cheese spread on the inside of the hollow toy or bone, stuff the bone with meat scraps, or put kibble in the cube and your dog will think of nothing else but working the object to get at the food. Great to take your dog's mind off the fact that you've left the house.

the dog immediately before the dog's good times and during the dog's good times. For example, ask your dog to sit and/or lie down each time before opening doors, serving meals, offering treats and tummy rubs; ask the dog to perform a few controlled doggy push-ups before letting her off leash or throwing a tennis ball; and perhaps request the dog to sit-down-sit-stand-down-stand-rollover before inviting her to cuddle on the couch.

Similarly, request the dog to sit many times during play or on walks, and in no time at all the dog will be only too pleased to follow your instructions because she has learned that a compliant response heralds all sorts of goodies. Basically all you are trying to teach the dog is how to say please: "Please throw the tennis ball. Please may I snuggle on the couch."

Remember, it is important to keep training interludes short and to have many short sessions each and every day. The shortest (and most useful) session comprises asking the dog to sit and then go play during a play session. When trained this way, your dog will soon associate training with good times. In fact, the dog may be unable to distinguish between training and good times and, indeed, there should be no distinction. The warped concept that training involves forcing the dog to comply and/or dominating her will is totally at odds with the picture of a truly well-trained dog. In reality, enjoying a game of training with a dog is no different from enjoying a game of backgammon or tennis with a friend; and walking with a dog should be no different from strolling with a spouse, or with buddies on the golf course.

WALK BY YOUR SIDE

Many people attempt to teach a dog to heel by putting her on a leash and physically correcting the dog when she makes mistakes. There are a number of things seriously wrong with this approach, the first being that most people do not want precision heeling; rather, they simply want the dog to follow or walk by their side. Second, when physically restrained during "training," even though the dog may grudgingly mope by your side when "handcuffed" on leash, let's see what happens when she is off leash. History! The dog is in the next county because she never enjoyed walking with you on leash and you

have no control over her off leash. So let's just teach the dog off leash from the outset to want to walk with us. Third, if the dog has not been trained to heel, it is a trifle hasty to think about punishing the poor dog for making mistakes and breaking heeling rules she didn't even know existed. This is simply not fair! Surely, if the dog had been adequately taught how to heel, she would seldom make mistakes and hence there would be no need to correct the dog. Remember, each mistake and each correction (punishment) advertise the trainer's inadequacy, not the dog's. The dog is not stubborn, she is not stupid and she is not bad. Even if she were, she would still require training, so let's train her properly.

Let's teach the dog to enjoy following us and to want to walk by our side off leash. Then it will be easier to teach high-precision off-leash heeling patterns if desired. Before going on outdoor walks, it is necessary to teach the dog not to pull. Then it becomes easy to teach on-leash walking and heeling because the dog already wants to walk with you, she is familiar with the desired walking and heeling positions and she knows not to pull.

FOLLOWING

Start by training your dog to follow you. Many puppies will follow if you simply walk away from them and maybe click your fingers or chuckle. Adult dogs may require additional enticement to stimulate them to follow, such as a training lure or, at the very least, a lively trainer. To teach the dog to follow: (1) keep walking and (2) walk away from the dog. If the dog attempts to lead or lag, change pace; slow down if the dog forges too far ahead, but speed up if she lags

too far behind. Say "Steady!" or "Easy!" each time before you slow down and "Quickly!" or "Hustle!" each time before you speed up, and the dog will learn to change pace on cue. If the dog lags or leads too far, or if she wanders right or left, simply walk quickly in the opposite direction and maybe even run away from the dog and hide.

Practicing is a lot of fun; you can set up a course in your home, yard or park to do this. Indoors, entice the dog to follow upstairs, into a bedroom, into the bathroom, downstairs, around the living room couch, zigzagging between dining room chairs and into the kitchen for dinner. Outdoors, get the dog to follow around park benches, trees, shrubs and along walkways and lines in the grass. (For safety outdoors, it is advisable to attach a long line on the dog, but never exert corrective tension on the line.)

Remember, following has a lot to do with attitude—your attitude! Most probably your dog will not want to follow Mr. Grumpy Troll with the personality of wilted lettuce. Lighten up—walk with a jaunty step, whistle a happy tune, sing, skip and tell jokes to your dog, and she will be right there by your side.

Your dog will quickly learn that the appearance of a leash means the arrival of a long-awaited trip outdoors.

84

BY YOUR SIDE

It is smart to train the dog to walk close on one side or the other—either side will do, your choice. When walking, jogging or cycling, it is generally bad news to have the dog suddenly cut in front of you. In fact, I train my dogs to walk "By my side" and "Other side"— both very useful instructions. It is possible to position the dog fairly accurately by looking to the appro-priate side and clicking your fingers or slapping your thigh on that side. A precise positioning may be at-tained by holding a training lure, such as a chew toy, tennis ball, or food treat. Stop and stand still several times throughout the walk, just as you would when window shopping or meeting a friend. Use the lure to make sure the dog slows down and stays close whenever you stop.

When teaching the dog to heel, we generally want her to sit in heel position when we stop. Teach heel po-sition at the standstill and the dog will learn that the default heel posi-tion is sitting by your side (left or right—your choice, unless you wish to compete in obedience trials, in which case the dog must heel on the left).

Several times a day, stand up and call your dog to come and sit in heel position—"Fido, heel!" For example, instruct the dog to come to heel each time there are commercials on TV, or each time you turn a page of a novel, and the dog will get it in a single evening.

Practice straight-line heeling and turns separately. With the dog sitting at heel, teach her to turn in place. After each quarter-turn, half-turn or full turn in place, lure the dog to sit at heel. Now it's time for short straight-line heeling sequences, no more than a few steps at a time. Always think of heeling in terms of sit-heel-sit sequences—start and end with the dog in position and do your best to keep her there when moving. Progressively increase the number of steps in each sequence. When the dog remains close for 20 yards of straight-line heeling, it is time to add a few turns and then sign up for a happy-heeling obedience class to get some advice from the experts.

NO PULLING ON LEASH

You can start teaching your dog not to pull on leash anywhere—in front of the television or outdoors—but

Beagles, like all dogs, will need to have their abundant energy and curiosity reigned in by efficient training.

neck will be traumatized for years to come.

Stand still and wait for the dog to stop pulling, and to sit and/or lie down. All dogs stop pulling and sit eventually. Most take only a couple of minutes; the all-time record is 22½ minutes. Time how long it takes. Gently praise the dog when she stops pulling, and as soon as she sits, enthusiastically praise the dog and take just one step forwards, then immediately stand still. This single step usually demonstrates the ballistic reinforcing nature of pulling on leash; most dogs explode to the end of the leash, so be prepared for the strain. Stand firm and wait for the dog to sit again. Repeat this half a dozen times and you will probably notice a progressive reduction in the force of the dog's one-step explosions and a radical reduction in the time it takes for the dog to sit each time.

regardless of location, you must not take a single step with tension in the leash. For a reason known only to dogs, even just a couple of paces of pulling on leash is intrinsically motivating and diabolically rewarding. Instead, attach the leash to the dog's collar, grasp the other end firmly with both hands held close to your chest, and stand still—do not budge an inch. Have somebody watch you with a stopwatch to time your progress, or else you will never believe this will work and so you will not even try the exercise, and your shoulder and the dog's

As the dog learns "Sit we go" and "Pull we stop," she will begin to walk forward calmly with each single step and automatically sit when you stop. Now try two steps before you stop. Wooooooo! Scary! When the dog has mastered two steps at a time, try for three. After each success, progressively increase the number of steps in the sequence.

CHAPTER NINE

Resources

BOOKS

About Beagles

Musladin, Judith M., MD, and A.C. Musladin, MD, and Ada Lueke. *The New Beagle*. New York: Howell Book House, 1990.

Vriends-Parent, Lucia. *Beagles: A Complete Pet Owner's Manual*. Hauppauge, NY: Barron's Educational Series, 1987.

About Health Care

American Kennel Club. *American Kennel Club Dog Care and Training*. New York: Howell Book House, 1991.

Carlson, Delbert, DVM, and James Giffen, MD. *Dog Owner's Home Veterinary Handbook*. New York: Howell Book House, 1992.

DeBitetto, James, DVM, and Sarah Hodgson. *You & Your Puppy*. New York: Howell Book House, 1995.

Lane, Marion. *The Humane Society of the United States Complete Guide to Dog Care*. New York: Little, Brown & Co., 1998.

McGinnis, Terri. *The Well Dog Book*. New York: Random House, 1991.

Schwartz, Stephanie, DVM. *First Aid for Dogs: An Owner's Guide to a Happy Healthy Pet*. New York: Howell Book House, 1998.

Volhard, Wendy and Kerry L. Brown. *The Holistic Guide for a Healthy Dog*. New York: Howell Book House, 1995.

About Training

Ammen, Amy. *Training in No Time*. New York: Howell Book House, 1995.

Benjamin, Carol Lea. *Mother Knows Best.* New York: Howell Book House, 1985.

Bohnenkamp, Gwen. *Manners for the Modern Dog.* San Francisco: Perfect Paws, 1990.

Dunbar, Ian, Ph.D., MRCVS. *Dr. Dunbar's Good Little Book.* James & Kenneth Publishers, 2140 Shattuck Ave. #2406, Berkeley, CA 94704. (510) 658-8588. Order from Publisher.

Evans, Job Michael. *People, Pooches and Problems.* New York: Howell Book House, 1991.

Palika, Liz. *All Dogs Need Some Training.* New York: Howell Book House, 1997.

Volhard, Jack and Melissa Bartlett. *What All Good Dogs Should Know: The Sensible Way to Train.* New York: Howell Book House, 1991.

About Activities

Hall, Lynn. *Dog Showing for Beginners.* New York: Howell Book House, 1994.

O'Neil, Jackie. *All About Agility.* New York: Howell Book House, 1998.

Simmons-Moake, Jane. *Agility Training, The Fun Sport for All Dogs.* New York: Howell Book House, 1991.

Vanacore, Connie. *Dog Showing: An Owner's Guide.* New York: Howell Book House, 1990.

Volhard, Jack and Wendy. *The Canine Good Citizen.* New York: Howell Book House, 1994.

MAGAZINES

THE AKC GAZETTE, The Official Journal for the Sport of Purebred Dogs
American Kennel Club
260 Madison Ave.
New York, NY 10016
www.akc.org

DOG FANCY
Fancy Publications
3 Burroughs
Irvine, CA 92618
(714) 855-8822
http://dogfancy.com

DOG WORLD
Maclean Hunter Publishing Corp.
500 N. Dearborn, Ste. 1100
Chicago, IL 60610
(312) 396-0600
www.dogworldmag.com

PETLIFE: Your Companion Animal Magazine
Magnolia Media Group
1400 Two Tandy Center
Fort Worth, TX 76102
(800) 767-9377
www.petlifeweb.com

DOG & KENNEL
7-L Dundas Circle
Greensboro, NC 27407
(336) 292-4047
www.dogandkennel.com

MORE INFORMATION ABOUT BEAGLE

National Breed Club

NATIONAL BEAGLE CLUB
Susan Mills Stoue, Secretary
2555 Pennsylvania NW
Washington, DC 20037

The Club can send you information on all aspects of the breed, including the names and addresses of breed clubs in your area, as well as obedience clubs. Inquire about membership.

The American Kennel Club

The American Kennel Club (AKC), devoted to the advancement of purebred dogs, is the oldest and largest registry organization in this country. Every breed recognized by the AKC has a national (parent) club. National clubs are a great source of information on your breed. The affiliated clubs hold AKC events and use AKC rules to hold performance events, dog shows, educational programs, health clinics and training classes. The AKC staff is divided between offices in New York City and Raleigh, North Carolina. The AKC has an excellent web site that provides information on the organization and all AKC-recognized breeds. The address is **www.akc.org**.

For registration and performance events information, or for customer service, contact:

THE AMERICAN KENNEL CLUB
5580 Centerview Dr., Suite 200
Raleigh, NC 27606
(919) 233-9767

The AKC's executive offices and the AKC Library (open to the public) are at this address:

THE AMERICAN KENNEL CLUB
260 Madison Ave.
New York, New York 10014
(212) 696-8200 (general information)
(212) 696-8246 (AKC Library)
www.akc.org

UNITED KENNEL CLUB
100 E. Kilgore Rd.
Kalamazoo, MI 49001-5598
(616) 343-9020
www.ukcdogs.com

AMERICAN RARE BREED
ASSOCIATION
9921 Frank Tippett Rd.
Cheltenham, MD 20623
(301) 868-5718 (voice or fax)
www.arba.org

CANADIAN KENNEL CLUB
89 Skyway Ave., Ste. 100
Etobicoke, Ontario
Canada M9W 6R4
(416) 675-5511
www.ckc.ca

ORTHOPEDIC FOUNDATION
FOR ANIMALS (OFA)
2300 E. Nifong Blvd.
Columbia, MO 65201-3856
(314) 442-0418
www.offa.org/

Trainers

Animal Behavior & Training Associates (ABTA)
9018 Balboa Blvd., Ste. 591
Northridge, CA 91325
(800) 795-3294
www.Good-dawg.com

Association of Pet Dog Trainers (APDT)
(800) PET-DOGS
www.apdt.com

National Association of Dog Obedience Instructors (NADOI)
729 Grapevine Highway, Ste. 369
Hurst, TX 76054-2085
www.kimberly.uidaho.edu/nadoi

Associations

Delta Society
P.O. Box 1080
Renton, WA 98507-1080
(Promotes the human/animal bond
through pet-assisted therapy and
other programs)
**www.petsform.com/DELTASOCIETY/
dsi400.htm**

Dog Writers Association
of America (DWAA)
Sally Cooper, Secretary
222 Woodchuck Lane
Harwinton, CT 06791
www.dwaa.org

National Association for Search
and Rescue (NASAR)
4500 Southgate Place, Ste. 100
Chantilly, VA 20157
(703) 222-6277
www.nasar.org

Therapy Dogs International
6 Hilltop Rd.
Mendham, NJ 07945

OTHER USEFUL RESOURCES— WEB SITES

General Information— Links to Additional Sites, On-Line Shopping

www.k9web.com – resources for the dog
world

www.netpet.com – pet related products,
software and services

www.apapets.com – The American Pet
Association

www.dogandcatbooks.com – book catalog

www.dogbooks.com – on-line bookshop

www.animal.discovery.com/ – cable
television channel on-line

Health

www.avma.org – American Veterinary
Medical Association (AVMA)

www.avma.org/care4pets/avmaloss.htm –
AVMA site dedicated to consideration of euthanizing sick pets and the
grieving process after losing a pet.

www.aplb.org – Association for Pet Loss
Bereavement (APLB)—contains an
index of national hot lines for on-line
and office counseling.

**www.netfopets.com/AskTheExperts.
html** – veterinary questions answered
on-line.

Breed Information

www.bestdogs.com/news/ – newsgroup

www.cheta.net/connect/canine/breeds/ –
Canine Connections Breed Information Index